STAGE SCHOOL

For Cathy Miyata,
my favourite drama consultant

ORCHARD BOOKS
96 Leonard Street, London EC2A 4XD
Orchard Books Australia
14 Mars Road, Lane Cove, NSW 2066
ISBN 1 86039 898 7
First published in Great Britain in 1999
Paperback original
Text © Sylvia McNicoll 1999
The right of Sylvia McNicoll to be identified as the author of
this work has been asserted by her in accordance with the
Copyright, Designs and Patents Act, 1988.
A CIP catalogue record for this book is available
from the British Library.
1 3 5 7 9 10 8 6 4 2
Printed in Great Britain

STAGE SCHOOL

★ Jenna ★
Standing Tall

by Geena Dare

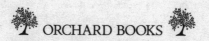

ORCHARD BOOKS

☆CHAPTER ONE☆

The Promise

Jenna ran hard through the inky black darkness toward the blazing white light, arms pumping, blue nightgown and dark hair streaming behind her. Even though she was fit from long hours of dancing, her mouth dropped open as she sucked in ragged breaths.

She put on a burst of speed and, as she passed Abbi and Dan, Jenna couldn't resist turning slightly to see how they were doing. They struggled too; Abbi in a nightgown almost identical to Jenna's, Dan in pale, striped pyjamas. Abbi's blue eyes looked as round and bright as headlights, and Dan's ears glowed red from his adrenaline rush. Jenna had never seen her friends look so frightened.

Hadn't they run from a fire in exactly this way only a couple of weeks ago? Only this time the fear on their faces seemed more intense. It was all too close, too real.

Jenna glanced back towards Matt, her dance partner. Pale and thin from his recent bout of glandular fever – the 'kissing disease' as they called it – still he ran as hard as Jenna, his worn grey dressing gown flapping open as he pushed against the wind. Bare-chested and wearing only his striped pyjama bottoms, he looked so vulnerable that Jenna wanted to throw her arms around him and keep him safe. It was a new, terrifying feeling for her, this wanting to protect him. Just because I need him for the New York workshop, she reasoned with herself; but deep down she knew that wasn't really all there was to it.

Suddenly, someone behind them screamed, sending cold fingers of shock down Jenna's spine. "Tanya's trapped in the dorm!"

Matt turned and tore back into the darkness. Jenna reached for him, a sob catching in her throat. "No, no don't! You'll never make it out of there alive."

"Cut!" a loud voice called from a megaphone. "That was almost perfect. Tall girl in the back..." The man behind the megaphone snapped his fingers at Jenna. "You're turning to look behind all the time. Let's take a break and we'll try it one more time."

The gang from the William S. Holly School of Performing Arts, affectionately known as Hollywood High by its students, had been hired as extras, or 'background performers' in a new film. It was the twentieth time the director had shot this scene. The first few times he'd been unhappy with the lighting. Then he'd spotted Matt wearing a digital watch, which hadn't even been invented back at the time of the story. Another time a screen had crashed down on the set. Over and over they'd performed the same scene.

Matt doubled over, shaking his head. "It'll never be right."

"I...I'm sorry," Jenna offered. "I ruined it for everyone. I'm just no good at this acting stuff."

"You're fine. We're all tired." Abbi rubbed her arms and shivered. Through this whole scene, Abbi, the aspiring actress from the Hollywood gang, had, of course, performed perfectly.

"Are you okay?" Dan asked Abbi. He was also a would-be actor from William S. Holly, and Abbi's close friend. "This is so much like the Maxwell Theatre fire, I don't even have to act."

She nodded. "But not half as bad, really. For me the worst part of that fire was being trapped in the passage under the stage. I thought we'd never get out alive. I'm remembering and reliving those feelings for this scene."

"Yeah, me too," Dan said. "Kind of wipes you out, doesn't it?"

"At least they're not setting you on fire," Matt shuddered. "I'll never forget when Blair pushed Abbi down into the snow to put out the flames on her mime costume."

"But we're using those awful memories, making the best of them," Abbi said. "That has to make us the perfect actors for this scene."

Jenna didn't feel perfect at all. Why had she turned to look at Abbi and Dan, and then again at Matt? This film stuff was confusing. She was a dancer not an actor! She hated feeling so out of control! They were running from a burning building, but the building itself wasn't there. A small model building would be set on fire later, and through computer generation be placed in the scene behind them.

The scenes themselves were filmed totally out of sequence so that she couldn't get any sense of the story. Night scenes were shot together. Scenes requiring the two stars, Levi Benson and Rebecca Tye, were filmed at the same time. Jenna had never even seen either of them, although she'd spotted Rebecca's double resting on a chair near the trailer between shots.

Before a shoot, the director had to explain what was happening and exactly where and when he wanted them to move or react. What did she know about motivation and reaction? Even the test reading of the script had been difficult – foreign-looking to her, with all its set and camera directions. Why had she even tried out as an extra? *Background performer,* she corrected herself, and sighed. Her passion was dancing and none of this filming had anything to do with that. She looked around at her friends from William Holly. They were the reason she was here. They had dragged her to the auditions. It would be good experience and fun, they had reasoned.

Lauren, the singer of their group, stepped into the light. Her face and hair were covered in soot. A long wig, which appeared singed at the ends, covered her short blonde bob.

Jenna thought she noticed Lauren's glance over at Matt. They'd gone out together briefly but they'd split up now, and Jenna knew *she'd* been the cause of her closest friend's heartbreak. But she didn't know how to change anything. It was just too bad that the two friends had to like the same boy – although it made sense in some ways; friends often had similar tastes.

Lauren had had some problems with the script, just like Jenna, but now she was adapting beautifully. She played the part of the young Tanya, the girl who needed to recover from her burns to go on and become a famous singing star. Rebecca Tye played the part of the adult Tanya.

"Hey, everyone! There's pizza over here," Lauren called.

The rich, spicy smell of tomato sauce and pepperoni wafted around Jenna and her mouth watered. She walked with the other extras towards the portable table set up in front of the trailer.

There were blue boxes full of ice and cans of drinks. She foraged in one for a diet soda. Orange, cola, lemonade, everything with sugar. She was so thirsty she wanted to grab one of the ice cubes to suck on instead of drinking all those calories.

Dan grabbed a piece of pizza and bit it, the cheese strings hanging down his chin. *"Mmm. Good."*

"Everything tastes good to you," Abbi commented. "Where do you put it all?"

Dan touched the back of his head as though preening. Then in a falsetto voice he said: "A minute on the lips, and a lifetime on the hips."

The others all laughed as they dug in too. Only

Jenna hesitated, actually thinking about what he was saying. It was true. Junk food only tasted good for a little while and then it sat on your body forever. And dancers couldn't afford pizza hips, or thighs or arms, for that matter.

"Come on, Jenna, have some," Matt coaxed. "Pizza's supposed to be the most nutritional fast food there is."

She had to drink something so she grabbed a can. Then she eyed the huge triangles of pizza, trying to find the smallest. She resigned herself to a slab that drooped over her hand, it was so big. It must have a ton of fat and calories in it, she thought. Nevertheless, she bit in and closed her eyes. *Mmmm*. It was the best pizza she'd ever tasted.

"Hey, everybody!" Shawn Siamon called. He was the producer and a former student of Hollywood High. "I want you to meet a friend of mine." His arm was draped round a fragile-looking woman with bones that seemed to push out of her skin.

Jenna stopped chewing the pizza. Was it really her? It couldn't be! She'd never even had a chance to see her perform, but Jenna had read and heard so much about her – and now she was standing right in front of her, in person.

The woman smiled vacantly as Shawn introduced her, her green eyes startling against her caramel coloured skin.

"This is Celine Laporte, the National Ballet's rising young star." Celine nodded at the group.

"She has consented to do a cameo performance in the variety show scene. This means we're looking for some dancers. We'll be filming it at the end of the month. Any of you dance classical ballet?"

Jenna swallowed quickly but choked on a piece of pepperoni as other hands shot up to volunteer.

"We both do!" Matt answered as he slapped Jenna's back.

Shawn motioned to his assistant who walked around taking down names on her clipboard.

She eyed Jenna. "You dance ballet? Gosh, you're big."

Jenna's cheeks burned.

Matt rose to her defence. "Jenna's the best dancer at our school." He put a hand on her shoulder and smiling warmly, pushed her forward. "We've won a scholarship to a New York workshop together."

The production assistant raised her eyebrows and shook her head. "Maybe so, but the costumes we've borrowed from the National Ballet are all size small. I assumed that most ballerinas were that size."

While the assistant jotted down the names of the other dancers, Jenna was trying hard to blink back tears, and she put down her pizza and her drink.

"Come on, Jenna. You're tired and hungry." Matt spoke softly to her and touched her arm. "You have to eat something. Don't let her get you down."

Jenna yanked her arm away. "I've worked hard

at watching my weight. I've dieted since December to make sure I won't grow any more."

"But that's stupid!" Matt hissed at her.

"Maybe. But I can't let one size end it for me."

She rushed after the assistant who stood near the wardrobe trailer looking over her clipboard. "Um, Miss?" She tapped the woman gingerly on the shoulder.

"What is it?" the woman asked in a tired voice as she turned.

Jenna words rushed out quickly. "I'm Jenna James and I'd really like to be added to your list! If the shoot's in a month, I promise I'll fit into the costume by then."

☆CHAPTER TWO☆

A New World

"I know you've been sick and I'm trying to be patient. But in order to stay at William S. Holly you need to maintain a B in all subjects. And, Matt Caruso, you're failing in English."

Matt frowned back at Mrs Colter. The essay she'd just handed him had received the lowest grade of his life and deserved it too, he knew that. He'd fallen behind when he was sick, and now that he was well, he found it too hard to sit still and read the books and then write up the reports and essays. Music pounded in his blood and he needed to get up and move to it. If only he could dance while he was reading or writing, instead of being bolted to one spot, he knew he could pull up his failing grades.

"You'll need to make up this assignment. See me at lunch time and we'll discuss it further," she said as she continued handing out papers.

"Mrs Colter, I can't come at lunch! I have dance practice." Matt put on his best apologetic smile. "Can I just make it up next assignment?"

"No, Matt." She waved her other papers at him

in a warning gesture. "See me after school, please."

"Yes, Mrs Colter."

Then Mrs Colter handed Jenna her essay, and Matt watched Jenna's blank expression change into one of horror.

"This can't be right, Mrs Colter!" she gasped as she looked at her grade. "I worked really hard on my Karen Kain paper."

"It just wasn't up to your usual standard. I know you think Miss Kain is 'the coolest, best, most talented ballet dancer'," Mrs Colter smiled. "But you didn't substantiate your opinions."

"But they're not just opinions; they're well-known facts," Jenna protested. "Her handprints are in cement on King Street. She's the only ballet dancer to be there."

"None of those things are 'well-known' to me," Mrs Colter said. "You might have included that handprint detail in your essay, Jenna."

Jenna frowned, rapping her fingers on her desk. "Can I do it again, like Matt? I like to keep my grades high."

Mrs Colter sighed. "It's just one B, Jenna, but very well, you can see me after school too."

Jenna looked this upset over a B! Matt almost laughed out loud but he knew that she would really blow up at him if he did. She never thought he was serious enough.

The lunch bell rang and Matt tried cheering Jenna up as they headed to the canteen. "Don't worry. We'll work on our grades together." At least that cheered *him* up. Matt would have loved to take Jenna out for pizza, or a movie, but everyone knew she was strictly all dance and school. The only time he could ever spend with her was work time. So what if dance was a pleasure as well as their chosen life discipline? That's how he could spend time with Jenna. Now Matt could spend more time with her by working on their English assignments together.

He rushed ahead of Jenna to their usual canteen table, hoping to keep enough places for their gang. Since Central Tech High burned down last term, three hundred art students had invaded William S. Holly. Now finding enough chairs at the canteen or in the library for that matter, was always a race.

"Matt! Over here!" Dan waved and Matt rushed over. They spread their books and bags all over the table to discourage the art student invaders.

"Nikki! Over here!" Dan called.

Matt shook his head. Only a girl as cute as Nikki could turn Dan into a traitor. Nikki was a petite artist with spiky black hair and puppy dog eyes. And she was easy-going, not prickly and highly strung, like Jenna. Matt sighed.

Dan opened his plastic container to reveal a steaming red and green mass of something.

"Ah, moussaka again?" Matt asked. "Is your dad still working on the novel with the Greek setting?" It seemed Dan's entire life was ruled by the nationality of the characters in his father's stories. It was like method acting, only his dad was a writer.

"Still? It hasn't been that long. Have you ever

tried moussaka before? Here, have some?" He held out a forkful but Matt backed away quickly. "It's good with ketchup and mustard too."

"I'll try," Nikki offered and slipped the fork into her mouth. "Sort of like lasagna with an attitude. I like it."

She would, Matt thought. There wasn't anything about Dan she didn't like.

"What's good?" Jenna asked as she sat down.

"Moussaka," Dan mumbled through his mouthful. "Hey, what do you have there, Jenna?"

Jenna unwrapped something that looked vaguely like a tortilla. Matt thought he could detect a quick nose wrinkle on her part. "It's rôti, a dish from Grenada. My mother and sister have got into cooking and baking mode for my grandmother's visit."

"Sounds great. Can I try?"

Jenna shoved her lunch over to Dan who took a big bite. "Oh, oh, oh!" He waved his hand in front of his mouth. "Water, water!"

Nikki quickly passed him her carton of chocolate milk and he gulped some down.

"It's good," he gasped after he had quenched his thirst.

Then he pushed Jenna's lunch back.

"You keep it," Jenna said. "It's got a thirty per cent fat content, and five hundred calories a roll."

"I like it even more!" Dan said "Have my moussaka. It's totally vegetarian. Low fun... I mean fat."

Matt frowned, wanting to stop the swap. Jenna

needed some calories. Too late. She took Dan's dish and began cutting up the moussaka in small bits. Then she lined up the bits as though they were soldiers in an army. Everything in her life had to be in neat rows and under her control, Matt thought. Why did he feel such a strong urge to mess up those rows?

"Hey, Matt. Have you heard about the production deal the school's worked out with the local TV station?"

"No, what about it?" Matt started eating his own cheeseburger when he finally saw Jenna nibble some of Dan's moussaka.

"We won't have room for a production studio at Holly for who knows how long," Dan said. "But now we can take a mini course on TV production on site at Cablecity. During after school hours, though. But for an extra credit! The sign-up sheet's over on the notice board. First come first served."

"I'm going to sign up right away." Matt scraped back his chair.

"What?" Jenna slapped down her fork. "How will you find the time? You've got to catch up on your school work and build up your dance stamina...plus you need your rest."

"Dance means everything to me," Matt explained to Jenna, "but I can't dance forever." He thought he'd bring up Jenna's ballet heroes to help his argument. "Now that your friend Frank Augustyn has retired, he's producing ballet documentaries and Karen Kain stars in them."

"What? Retired! He's over forty years old," Jenna

said. "I'm sure he didn't work in films when he was your age. He concentrated on his form and movement."

"Mikhail Baryshnikov acted in that movie *Turning Point*. Do you know how many kids were turned on to ballet by that film? I think dance and media have a place together." Matt paused.

"Dan and I've signed up already," Nikki broke in helpfully. "We're applying the credit to our English class."

Matt stood up. "That's it, Jenna. Here's a way for you to get your A and me to get my pass grade."

Jenna chewed her lip and then rose slowly to join him. "If Mrs Colter approves, I guess it would be more fun than rewriting an essay."

"Come on. Let's go before the list fills up," he said to her happily. Television production could help their English grades but he also hoped it would loosen Jenna up, and open her up to new worlds. Perhaps the wonderful world of going out and having fun with him! He spun round with his arms high and then performed his best leap towards the notice board. But even as he signed his name, he noticed Jenna scraping most of Dan's moussaka into the garbage.

☆CHAPTER THREE☆

The Family Curse

"Ahh, you're just in time for callaloo." Jenna's sister Joyce held out a spoonful of the soup for her to taste. "It's so good."

Even though Joyce was older, she stood a head shorter than Jenna, which made Jenna wish she could switch bodies with her. Joyce wore a red and white T-shirt labelled 'Engineering Dept' with tight red jeans which really accentuated her soft curves. Joyce's body curved a little too softly for Jenna's purposes but dancing and dieting could fix that. Height was beyond her control, Jenna thought. Or was it? The health teacher at her last school had once warned that dieting could stunt your growth. If only, Jenna thought.

Joyce's spoon beckoned, temptingly. Jenna knew the soup was rich with crab meat and coconut milk but she also knew that she needed to fit into that ballet costume in a month. The production assistant had said she could rehearse for the Celine Laporte number, but if she couldn't squeeze into the costume for the shoot, she would be cut.

Jenna *could* control her appetite. The rest of her life was another matter.

She pushed the spoon away. "Is food all you people think about?"

Joyce slurped the soup up herself. "Mmm." She smacked her lips. "With Nana coming that's all anyone's going to think about for a month." She waved the spoon in the air. "It's going to be a Caribbean food fest. Whoohoo!"

"Jenna, are you coming to the airport?" Her mother called from the bathroom.

"Of course. I came home straight from school specially." At least, it had been directly after her meeting with Mrs Colter.

Jenna looked forward to her grandmother's visit. Nana James had taken her to her first ballet, *Giselle*, when Jenna was only six years old. Nana had some contacts in the National Ballet and had got them the best seats. "Back in Grenada, I used to dance in the same class as the woman who is now the Director," she'd explained to Jenna. "I got married but she continued on," Nana had sighed regretfully.

No one else had thought Jenna would be old enough to sit still. But Nana knew better and when Jenna instantly fell in love with ballet, Nana paid for dancing lessons. "No regrets for you, baby girl," she'd said. Her grandmother was always the one who had understood.

Her mother burst from the bathroom wearing one of her usual brightly-coloured dresses – this one was a large red cherry print on a yellow background. Jenna sighed. There was never anything subtle about her mother's clothes.

"Have some soup, honey," she called. "Who knows when we'll have supper?"

Jenna glanced over at the pot. "I'm stuffed. Matt gave me a muffin after school."

"Yes, that would certainly fill a person right up." Joyce rolled her eyes and smiled.

"Girls, help me," her mother pleaded. "Where are my car keys? Where's my bag?" Her mum rushed from room to room, frantically.

Joyce picked up a bag from the kitchen counter and a set of keys from the desk near the telephone. Then she stood in the hall and grinned till their mother noticed.

"Thank you. My glasses? Jenna, have you seen them?"

Standing together now, her mum and sister looked as bright as an Island fruit basket. In her dark blue turtleneck and skirt Jenna felt as though she was dressed for a funeral – the one celebrating the death of her film dance debut. With all the eating her family would be doing over the month, that's just what her grandmother's arrival could prove to be. Jenna sighed and pointed. "Your glasses are on your head, Mum."

Her mother pulled the large red frames down on to her face. "Come on, let's go, girls. Your grandmama awaits!"

Jenna grabbed her coat and followed her family out of the door.

As they drove, she worried about the

forthcoming feasting. Why did her family's celebrations always have to centre around food? Sometimes she felt sure they were purposely plotting to make her fat. After all, they didn't think dancing was a practical career, anyway. She had been so looking forward to Nana's visit too, only she knew now her family would use Nana as an excuse to turn every meal into a calorie blitz.

If only they had a dog, she thought, she could easily slip some of the excess food under the table. When they sat in the dining room, she might be able to dump some at the base of the large rubber tree, as long as the colour and texture blended with the soil. She would cut down on breakfast and lunch.

"That way, Mum." Joyce's driving instructions interrupted her thoughts. Her sister pointed to the road exit marked with an aeroplane sign. They drove along silently, Jenna marvelling at the planes she saw high above them. Any one of them might be carrying her grandmother. Any one of them might carry her and Matt to their New York dance workshop this spring break.

"Look! Foreign Arrivals." Joyce pointed again and the car turned up a ramp. "Parking's that way." With each twist and turn up the parking levels, Jenna's diet worries became increasingly replaced with anticipation and excitement.

She heard and felt the sounds and vibrations of jets taking off as they stepped out of the car and headed for Arrivals. She watched people lining up with suitcases as cars and cabs rolled up to the entrances to pick them up.

"The white zone is for immediate loading and unloading only," a voice warned over an intercom.

"We'll need to find out what gate she's coming from," her mother said as they strode up to a television monitor with the arrivals listed on it.

"Flight 737 Grenada Air, arrival time six thirty, gate number 43," her sister read.

The clock on the wall flashed 18:50. "The plane landed early. She's already here!" Jenna jumped a little, clapping her hands together. "Let's hurry."

They bustled through a crowd of suntanned tourists, pilots and flight attendants. Jenna searched above everyone's heads trying to catch a glimpse of her grandmother.

A flash of peacock blue, two bright blue earrings, a beaming brown face framed by closely cropped hair. Yes, yes that was her! She stood taller than everyone else in the crowd. Jenna rushed forward towards her.

Her grandmother grinned, dropped her bag on to her luggage trolley and threw open her arms in a welcome embrace. "Girl Child!" she shrieked and then wrapped her arms around her in a suffocating hug. "You've grown so-o-o big," she boomed.

Jenna cringed as the whole airport turned to see exactly who had grown "so-o-o big".

She'd always loved her Nana's voice. Her words floated like island music, making Jenna think of the ocean lapping on the beach and the winds singing in the palm trees. Today it sounded more like a hurricane.

Her grandmother stood back and eyed her. "But

you're nothing but skin and bones!" She poked a long finger into Jenna's ribs. "Grandma's got some work to do on you."

Then she turned to Joyce. "And how's the smartest engineering student in the country doin'?"

Joyce smiled as she took her turn hugging Nana. "Great! I got another A+ on a paper today."

Jenna wanted to brag about something too, but a B in English didn't measure up and Nana already knew about New York. As she grabbed her grandmother's overnight bag she thought about the extra credit that would pick up her mark. "I signed up for a television production course today, Nana."

"Jenna, that's exciting," her mother said, breaking from Nana James' hug. "It might lead to a job one day!"

"Dance class will lead to a job." Jenna flipped the canvas strap of the overnight bag over her shoulder.

"Dance is everything," Joyce explained to their grandmother, as she rolled her suitcase towards the door. "Do you know Jenna turned down a big modelling contract with the Lara Lake Agency?"

Grandma smiled at Jenna as they reached the car. "Really?"

Her mother unlocked the back and Jenna tossed the overnight bag in. "No, not really."

She'd never told her family that when she'd gone to the test shoot and she'd found herself alone in the strangest circumstances with Norman Mars, the photographer who'd spotted her. He hadn't been in a position to offer her a contract at all and all the photos on his walls had been of girls in skimpy underwear.

"Jenna's just being all modest," Joyce said as she loaded the rest of the suitcases into the boot. "If I were as skinny as she was, I'd certainly have signed. Could have paid my entire tuition fees just prancing around in some fancy clothes."

Jenna slammed down the back.

Nana opened the car door and stood for a moment clicking her tongue. "You should be takin' advantage, Girl Child. All the James' girls start off as scrawny as you. We shoot up, we're tall, then we fill out."

Jenna watched as her mother and sister climbed into their seats. It was true. They weren't exactly *fat*, but they were definitely shapely.

Jenna blinked for a moment, trying to imagine beautiful Celine Laporte with a rounded figure like any of the women in her family. She shook her head to clear the picture. Filling out was something Jenna could not afford to do.

☆CHAPTER FOUR☆

A No-Show

The next night, Jenna's mother nagged her to eat up all her supper.

"But I'm full, Mum. I couldn't possibly eat any more." She said after a couple of mouthfuls. She held her stomach with one hand convincing even herself.

"You're working too hard and getting too thin. Relax," her mother told her. "Stay at the table for a while, maybe you'll be able to eat a little more that way."

"But Mum, I'm trying out for a dancing part in Shawn Siamon's movie—" she started to explain.

"What's this?" her grandmother jumped in. "My granddaughter's goin' to be some fancy movie star?" She rolled her eyes and grinned.

"Last week she had to pretend she was an orphan running from a burning building," her mother offered.

"My goodness. Such an excitin' life – modellin', television production, actin'." Her grandmother listed off all the things that didn't matter to Jenna, that she wasn't really good at. Why didn't she include dance? She, of all people should have understood. Jenna knew her mother and sister didn't understand or accept her dedication to dance. But Nana? Jenna felt betrayed.

"Stop that playin' with your food," her grandmother said when Jenna lined up her peas neatly beside her rice. Nana passed round a plate of guava and nutmeg jellies she'd brought with her from the Island. On top of that, she produced a chocolate cake with eight layers of butter icing sandwiched in between. "Special German recipe," she winked. "I bought it myself at the bakery this afternoon."

Jenna eyed the cake as though it was a chocolate tank. She clenched and unclenched her fists under the table as the smell of chocolate intoxicated her. If she could only resist this, she would win one small fight in her daily war to be the cleverest, most graceful and talented – and the thinnest. She wanted to show that she was more clever than her sister Joyce, she wasn't going into ballet just to escape academic courses at university. She wanted to prove she was more graceful and talented than the giggling girls in her dance class – she could always work harder and longer than they did. She wanted to be more thin than... she thought about that one for a moment and the image of the beautiful, fragile-looking Celine Laporte danced into her mind. Yes, she would be thinner than Celine. Her bones would stick out in just the same way that made Celine's face so angular and intriguing. She wondered exactly how much Celine weighed.

"I'm too full for cake," Jenna said, feeling some satisfaction at the way her grandma's mouth dropped. Her nana of all people should have known a ballet dancer couldn't eat cake. So it had to be true, Nana wasn't on her side any more.

"I'm going to go do some homework now." Then she rushed to the computer to search the internet for information on her new heroine, Celine Laporte.

She found out all the ballets Celine had danced in, and all the partners she'd danced with. She saw that Celine Laporte sometimes made school visits too. Maybe she could ask Miss Adaman to invite her. But skimming through the material, she couldn't find any details of Celine's weight. Something else caught her eye, though. Before Celine Laporte had joined the National Ballet, she had loved jogging along the lake to keep fit as well as to get rid of stress. That was it! Her mother had forced her to eat too much at supper but now she would jog those calories off. Just like Celine Laporte.

Jenna quickly shut down her internet connection and headed for her bedroom to change into a tracksuit. Then she made a dash for the door when no one was looking. Down the hall and into the elevator and out on to the street, safe and free from her mother, sister and grandmother and all that food.

Jenna's feet pounded the pavement. She kept her arms bent at right angles and her fists punched out with each stride. The rhythm of her heart and her feet seemed in perfect harmony. It was almost like a dance, really, very satisfying. Thump, thump, thump, thump. She made sure to skip the cracks in the path. *Step on a crack, break your mother's back*, the childhood chant came back to her. Just a stupid rhyme; still, Jenna wouldn't take any chances, her dad after all had died when she was six years old. She looked straight ahead now, concentrating on her breathing. She didn't take chances with anything – extra food or weight. She liked to control things. So why did she have the feeling there was something she was forgetting? Was it that stupid French homework, she wondered. She could leave that for one night as she worked off the dinner's calories. That couldn't be what was bothering her. It felt as though she was supposed to be somewhere else. Only where?

☆

Matt stood in awe behind the huge black camera sitting on the tripod in front of him. All this equipment! And he'd never seen such a cluttered ceiling before. Lights of all shapes and sizes hung down from it.

On the other side of the studio, Dan gave a low whistle as he walked around his camera. "Wow, these are just like the ones they're using to shoot Shawn Siamon's picture."

Nikki stood beside him. "This is so cool," she said, leaning close to peer through the viewfinder.

There were three cameras in the Cablecity studio, all aimed at a brightly lit set consisting of a desk, a huge jungle-like plant and a couch. A group of four William S. Holly students stood around each camera. Matt frowned. There should have been thirteen students. Jenna was late. Where was the well-disciplined ballerina today? he wondered critically.

"Welcome, everyone," Byron Jenson, the instructor of the television production class, called out as he stepped in front of the set. "The first thing I would like to teach you is some proper terminology. We do not film at this station; we 'videotape'. Film is something that needs to be developed." He smiled at the students. "Next, some safety rules." He walked over to Matt's camera and grabbed a wire. "Coil the cable hanging from the back of your camera into a figure of eight." He demonstrated with the wire. "It's neater, and hopefully prevents tripping."

Dan and Nikki immediately shaped the wire behind their shared camera into a neat eight.

Matt glanced nervously at the door. Jenna was never this late. Something must have happened. Should he run out and look for her?

"Where's Jenna?" Dan whispered to him. "Do you think she forgot about the workshop?"

Matt shook his head. "I reminded her at dance practice but she's been acting pretty spacey lately, with her grandmother visiting and all."

"Pay attention now!" Byron called. "This lever is the camera lock."

He went on to explain all the buttons and levers to the students. "Now look through your viewfinder and watch the colour bar. The camera's black and white so they won't actually appear in colour."

The stripes in the little window appeared to Matt as different shades of grey and black.

"We'll leave that on for a full minute to act as a control track for the automatic editor." Byron went on.

Next, he held a piece of white paper in front of Dan's camera. "This is how we test the white balance. Check the viewfinder and move the dial till you see a true white."

The students took turns adjusting the balance and then messing it up so the person behind them could try.

The three hour workshop sped by. Byron showed them how to zoom in on a subject, focus on their eyes and then zoom out again, staying in perfect focus. He demonstrated how to pan the camera slowly, so that watching it afterwards wouldn't make viewers feel dizzy. Then he showed them a video with different effects achieved by the various techniques. "Through the camera's eye, you will sometimes observe things that you never noticed before," he commented, as the video showed close-ups of different subjects.

Luckily, he didn't check attendance, because by the end of the class, Jenna still hadn't shown up. Matt felt hot and confused with worry and anger. Jenna had never forgotten anything before, and it was not like her to simply skip an activity once she had committed to it.

"Next week, we'll take turns as camera operators and subjects," Byron told them. "See you then."

Matt had hoped to approach Byron about his English project. Mrs Colter had agreed he could make up for one of his bad marks by taking the television course. They were studying media arts in English this term anyway, so he could make up for another bad mark by creating a video. Now he wanted some help – where to begin, how to get the best shots – but with Jenna not showing up, all his thoughts were taken up with her. She hadn't been that eager to join; had she decided not to come after all? Or had something happened to her? Should he simply invent some excuse for her and ask about an extra class to make up the one she had missed. He could even offer to lend her his own notes. Only they weren't very good and Jenna was so serious about stuff like that. He hesitated. Then a technician walked in and started talking to Byron and Matt knew he'd missed his chance.

The moment he stepped out of the studio, he spotted a telephone. He took a deep breath. Whether it was good or bad he needed to find out what had happened to Jenna. He keyed in her number. Someone picked up immediately.

"Hello, James' residence, Beverley James speakin'," a voice sang. Matt didn't recognize the voice; the lady had an accent. Had he dialled the wrong number?

"Come on, are you shy?" the voice asked.

"Are you Jenna's grandmother?" Matt asked awkwardly.

"I'll be doin' the askin', if you don't mind." Then she chuckled, putting Matt more at ease. "Who are you?"

"I'm Matt Caruso. Is Jenna there, please?" Matt didn't know how her grandmother felt about boys calling so he nervously introduced himself. "I'm her dance partner."

"Just a moment, please."

Matt heard her calling for Jenna loudly, at first, and then from farther away as though she were searching.

Finally, she returned to the phone, breathless. "I'm so sorry but I cannot find that girl anywhere. She was just eatin' with us a minute ago. That girl child never sits still."

Matt chewed his lip for a moment. If she'd sat down to eat with her only a moment ago, then Jenna must be OK. He didn't want to tell her grandmother about the missed television class in case that got Jenna into trouble.

"When I find her, shall I tell her you called?" she asked.

Where had Jenna gone? How could she have forgotten the class? It just wasn't like her. Finally he answered, "No, no. That's all right. I'll talk to her at school."

☆CHAPTER FIVE☆

The Tribal Beat

Next day at lunch, while the rest of the gang was at choir, drama or in the studio, Matt sat alone with Jenna. He watched her pick at a sandwich unhappily. "Come on Jenna. Don't be hard on yourself about it. Your grandmother's here, there's so much going on at your house. It was easy to forget the television production class."

She ripped the crust off the bread in tiny bits, as though she was going to feed it to the pigeons. "You reminded me after school and I remembered as I walked home. But when I stepped into the house there was all that smell of spicy food. And Mum made me eat so much. I went running to burn it all off and forgot all about the class." She broke one half of her sandwich into quarters. "Bread at lunch. I'd at least like to cut out the starch to make up for all those huge suppers I'm having."

It was as though television had slipped her mind again as she studied the little sandwich quarters. Matt puzzled over what she was doing. Jenna sure acted weird sometimes. Had she always done these strange things to her food? He couldn't recall.

"You could tell Mrs Colter you'll just accept your B," he continued, trying to soothe her. "Who knows, with all your other As maybe you'll keep your high average."

"Maybe?" Jenna glared up at him. "Maybe's not good enough for me. I'm not just some stupid dancer. My sister's going to be an engineer, you know."

"You've mentioned that a few times. So what? Listen, we'll ask Byron if I can help you catch up." Somewhere in Matt's mind he saw himself putting his arms around Jenna to demonstrate the camera lock, and tilt and focus. Somehow he could picture her melting from this hard knot of determination into the Jenna he had once kissed on the steps in front of the theatre. "It is only one class. We can tell him you were sick." Matt stopped when he noticed Jenna sweeping all the crumbs and sandwich quarters back into her lunch bag. "Jenna, are you OK?"

"Of course."

But she wasn't responding to his suggestions. Matt chewed his lip, confused and frustrated by her strange behaviour. "OK," he said finally, "let's go and practise."

They headed off to the dance studio together. Miss Adaman joined them on their way over, a tray of lunch in her hand. "You're here as usual. My dancing duo." She smiled.

As they stepped into the room, Miss Adaman

put the tray on a small table near the piano. Although Jenna's mind felt as though it was full of fuzz lately, her sense of smell had improved and she could identify what people were eating just by sniffing. There was chicken noodle soup in that bowl, she thought. A hint of bay leaf, a dash of garlic…

Jenna couldn't help staring at it. The overwhelming smell had begun to nauseate her. She tried breathing through her mouth to avoid it. She forced herself to think of something else, too: ballet, her heroine, anything. "Miss Adaman, do you know the ballet dancer Celine Laporte? It says on her internet biography that she makes school visits."

"That is true." Miss Adaman wiped her mouth with a napkin. "But she's on sick leave right now. Mr Rudolph already tried to book her."

"Sick leave? But she's appearing in Shawn Siamon's film. We're supposed to be rehearsing with her," Matt said.

"Lucky you. Perhaps she's just not up to the rigour of daily public performances." Miss Adaman shrugged. "Or facing artistic teenagers." She smiled. "But we *are* having some guest performers this afternoon. A special surprise. I'm sure you will enjoy them."

When Miss Adaman said 'you' she looked directly at Jenna, and Jenna felt a thrill shoot through her. William S. Holly hosted lots of visits by professional performers. Last term the Rhythmics visited their dance class. Miss Adaman knew how much Jenna loved ballet. If Celine Laporte wasn't available, maybe Mr Rudolph had found someone else from the ballet world. Jenna's hopes soared.

"Now hurry up if you want to get some practice in. I'm just going to finish my soup and return my bowl to the canteen."

Jenna felt all shivery with excitement as she performed the usual stretches, *pliés*, *petits battements* and *ports de bras*. When she stepped on to the floor to dance with Matt, though, she still felt too cold to shed her warm-up sweatsuit. She saw sweat shine on Matt's forehead as he lifted her with difficulty.

"I'm sure glad we don't have any of this macho hoisting stuff in our New York number," he complained as he set her down.

"Do you have a fever?" Jenna asked, wondering how he could be so hot when she wanted to turn up the heat.

"No. I'm just warm from lifting you!" he answered.

Jenna bit her lip. All that weight she'd lost since November and still she was too heavy for her partner to lift her.

Miss Adaman returned and stopped the music. "Please, towel off now. Our guests have arrived." She looked out of the studio door. "Welcome!" she called to the mystery guests.

They strode into the room, laughing and talking. There were five of them, all with skin colours ranging from deep olive to a burnt chocolate. One young man carried in a tall narrow drum. The other one hung up his coat in Miss Adaman's cloakroom and then came out stripped to the waist. The drummer took off his sweatshirt, too. The three young women took off their jackets to reveal brightly-patterned cotton wrap-style dresses. Around their hair they wound strips of cloth that matched their wraps.

Miss Adaman smiled. "Matt, Jenna, may I introduce The Tribal Beat. These young men and women perform African, Brazilian and West Indian dancing. This is Jamal, Miguel, Ellen, Kayla and Margaret." She pointed to Matt and Jenna now. "These are two of my best students – Matt and Jenna."

Why hadn't she invited ballet performers? Jenna wanted to shout. Then she felt other hard feelings boil up inside her. Of course Mrs Adaman would expect this dancing to appeal to her. She was just like all the others, thinking a tall black girl couldn't possibly make it in the ballet world. The Tribal Beat, however, was custom-made for Jenna.

"Good to meet you. Good to be here," Jamal and Miguel responded to the introductions. "Excuse us while we just warm up a bit," Miguel said to them.

The dancers removed their socks and then surprised Jenna by performing the same knee bends, leg stretches, foot beats and arm movements she did to warm up each day. The drummer flexed his wrists and flapped his hands as he jogged on the spot.

As the rest of the dance class drifted in and settled on a bench, Jake spoke to them as he began tapping his drum. "When black slaves were brought to the Americas, the rhythm and beat of their tribal music frightened their owners. It seemed like a kind of captivating magic." He drummed a little harder. "So of course it was outlawed." Jake stopped abruptly and then began again softly. "Still the black people managed to retain their culture by masking their dances as acceptable religious rites."

The other four dancers began shuffling in circles, their bare feet slapping the floor in time to the beat of the drum.

"After freedancing rhythmically, as they always did, people stumbled and swooned as though the spirit had entered them."

The drumming continued, the dancers shuffled faster. Suddenly one shuffled off beat, appeared to mis-step and then collapse.

Even though Jenna folded her arms across her chest determined not to be a part of any of this, she found her own foot tapping.

"Join us!" Jamal beckoned to Jenna.

She shook her head curtly. Matt glanced sidelong at her, his face screwed up in a puzzled expression. Then he stepped forward himself. He shuffled along naturally, his head bobbing to the beat, his feet slap-slapping. The drums beat louder and Jenna felt the rhythm throbbing at her temples, or was it her pulse? It was as though that drum pounded inside her somewhere. Other William

Holly students joined The Tribal Beat. The drumming quickened. Jenna felt something inside her race. Without meaning to, she shuffled in among the other dancers. She didn't just bob her head, she bent her torso at the waist – back and forth to the rhythm, her chin jabbing as though at some invisible drum.

Suddenly the guest dancers whirled around as they stamped their feet. Jenna joined them. She felt her face crack open into a wide smile. She couldn't help it. Faster and faster she spun. Suddenly, the room turned on a strange angle. She couldn't find the floor and she felt so light that she began floating away, only then her knees buckled under her and everything went dark.

The next thing she felt was Matt's arms lifting her up. "Hey, are you all right?" He guided her to one of the benches along the wall. "This swooning as-the-spirit-fills-you stuff doesn't seem healthy." He said it lightly enough but his brows furrowed as he scrutinised her face.

Jenna nodded and then smiled at his concern. She still felt absurdly light as though she was about to float away at any moment.

Miss Adaman gave her a glass of water. "How are you feeling?" The other dancers stood around her, still for once, in shocked silence.

"Fine," Jenna told her weakly. "A little strange, maybe."

"You better stay put for the rest of class," Miss. Adaman suggested.

"I'll keep her company," Matt offered.

Jenna shook her head. "No. Really, I'm fine. You've sat out enough dancing with your illness," she told him, referring to his bout of glandular fever.

"I'll sit with Jenna. Better drink the rest of that water, dear," Miss Adaman said as she sat down beside her.

Jenna sipped dutifully as she watched the rest of the dance. Matt glanced back at her from time to time, but then she could see the music took over him too. He looked oddly relaxed and comfortable with the primal dancing. She had to admit that before she'd fainted, she'd really got into it herself. Lucky Matt, though, she thought. He could dance and enjoy African folk dance without being pushed into it. Plus the ballet world really needed tall good-looking male dancers like him. No one would tell him he was too tall or too big.

At the end of the class, Jamal came up to Jenna. "I'm sorry you're not well, but you're very welcome to join us any time. We have an open house, every Sunday." He handed her and all the others a card. "We really have a lot of fun."

She took the card but shook her head. "I'm sorry, I don't think I have the time. I'm...uh...really very busy with my classical stuff."

☆CHAPTER SIX☆

The Force Feed

At the second television production class, Matt stopped wondering whether Jenna would show up. This time, Byron checked the class attendance at the beginning of the class, when he read out Jenna's name and got no response he immediately crossed it out with his marker pen.

Matt winced, then looked over at Dan who just shrugged. Jenna obviously didn't care enough about this class. But it was so unlike her to skip anything that Matt couldn't help worrying.

If he hadn't been so worried, Matt thought he would have really enjoyed this class. The lesson was fascinating and everyone was having fun. The students learned about the action axis and how cameras had to be placed, so as not to cross it. They also learned about framing a shot; keeping the skyline either one-third or two-thirds down the frame, making sure their eyes were one-third down the frame, andleaving more space in the direction a subject was speaking or moving.

Then they videoed each other in pairs at the desk, correctly and incorrectly. Matt felt uncomfortable without the other half of his usual team, so he just watched as Dan stuck a huge tropical plant behind Nikki. When Dan replayed his video, leaves appeared to be sprouting out from her head and ears. The students took turns in the control room, working the audio mixer and in the editing suite.

Matt only half-listened as Byron was talking to them about appearing on television. "Don't wear checks. They bleed. Stripes are no good. They appear to vibrate on the screen. Clunky jewellery interferes with mike reception, and while people think that white makes you look fatter, it actually brightens too much on the screen, making everything else around it, your face for example, look dingier," he said. He also announced that they were to sign up for the mobile cameras to do some practice shots.

Practice shots? Matt shook himself. Maybe he could use the real mobile unit instead of his family's camcorder to make the video for his English project. Matt still hadn't started it yet and Mrs Colter had been nagging him about it. He'd been counting on Jenna's help. She was always so terrific at school work, but he just couldn't get any interest out of her for this project. Now desperate, he hung back after class to ask Byron whether he could practise at the same time as shooting his project.

"That's a great idea, Matt. Call me when you want the camera and if it's not in use, you can borrow it. What's your movie about?" he said as he began walking towards his office.

"I haven't a clue." Matt blushed as he strode along beside him. "I thought I'd just video a bunch of stuff and hope for the best."

Byron shook his head. "A little thought saves a lot of work. Even a home movie is much better if you storyboard it. What are your interests?"

"Dance," Matt replied. And Jenna, he thought.

Byron looked at him. "Dance, eh? Well, what do you want to say about dance. You need to have an angle or a viewpoint, a theme of some sort." He hesitated outside his office now.

Matt shrugged his shoulders. *"Dance is Beautiful?"* he offered weakly, his head filling instantly with visions of Jenna on point.

"Something stronger, I think. How about: *Dance is Everything*, or better still, *Dance is Life.*"

Matt nodded enthusiastically. That theme seemed like something that would appeal to Jenna too. "I like that idea a lot. I wonder, do you suppose I could borrow the camera tonight? We're rehearsing a dance number with Celine Laporte and I'm hoping she'll let me video a little of it."

Byron raised an eyebrow and smiled. "Let's look at the list." He walked into his office and pulled a clipboard from his desk. "You're in luck, no one's booked in this evening. Is someone coming to pick you up?"

Matt pointed out of the window to the Caruso's Vegetables and Fruits van. "That's my mum now."

"All right. I'll get the camera for you." They headed for the storage room together and Byron gave him an extra battery pack and two tapes. "Take a lot of footage, Matt. You can use the editing suite to sort out what you want to keep." He draped the strap of the camera case over Matt's shoulder and stuffed the tripod under Matt's arm. "You're also going to need lighting." He buckled a belt around Matt. "This is a sun gun. It stays plugged into the battery pack on the belt but you mount it on the camera when you're at your location."

As he walked out of the building, he felt weighed down with equipment, as well as worry about Jenna. His mother's mouth dropped open as he approached. "These are expensive movie machines. Matteo, are you sure you will be able to look after them?"

"Sure." He loaded it all into the back of the truck. "Maybe we can lock the van in the garage while we eat, though."

When they rolled into the drive, Mrs Caruso pressed her remote control garage door opener. The van barely squeezed past Matt's sisters' and brother's bicycles. He leapt out immediately and ran into the house to call Jenna. He picked up the phone in the hall and dialled her number.

"Hello, James' residence. Beverley James speakin'." Jenna's grandmother again!

Matt thought about asking for Jenna and then thought better of it. What if he reminded her about the rehearsal tonight and then she spaced out again and forgot. This was too important. Maybe it was safer to leave a reminder with Jenna's grandmother. "Would you please tell her we're supposed to be at the Shawn Siamon ballet rehearsal in an hour?"

"When she gets in from her runnin', I will do that. Is this her dance partner again?" There was something mocking in that lilting voice.

"Yes, it is."

"I'm not certain she should be goin'. Her dance teacher called about her passin' out."

"Maybe if she eats something..." Whoops, it was out. Matt felt instantly disloyal, as though he was telling tales about her. "I mean, Mrs James, I don't think Jenna can pass up an opportunity to rehearse with Celine Laporte. It's just too important for her."

"You're a smart young man. I'm goin' to listen to you," her grandmother said. "Her mother and sister they be flittin' around. I can't ask their opinion when they're not here."

"Thank you ma'am." Matt felt relieved. He'd made his point without spoiling it for Jenna. She would be going. "Goodbye." He slipped the phone back into the cradle.

At that moment, Jenna was pounding along the side of the road enjoying the rhythm of her running. Three kilometres yesterday. Today she'd take a jog down a side street and add another kilometre. What was for supper tonight? Chicken, Nana had told her. If she took off the skin, didn't eat the potato alongside, she should be all right. As she jogged along, she wondered if she could get up earlier tomorrow morning and perhaps run a few more kilometres.

When she finally dashed back into the house, Nana called her into the kitchen. The table was already set. A huge salad sat at her place along with a plate full of chicken and a potato.

"You sit down and eat, Girl Child, every last bit."

Jenna opened her mouth to protest.

Her grandmother held up her hand. "You have no time to argue. You start eatin' and listen to me."

Jenna slipped into the chair and stabbed a lettuce leaf as though she were driving a stake through its heart.

"Your dance teacher called and said you fainted today."

"Nana, that was tribal dancing. I wasn't used to it. It's so wild and crazy—"

Her grandmother held up her hand again. "I'm talkin' now. You're supposed to be at a rehearsal with Celine Laporte in twenty minutes."

Jenna gasped. How could she have forgotten?

"Your mother's not around so I'm decidin' for her. You eat everything in front of you and you can go. Otherwise..."

"But I'll be too late!" Jenna protested.

"Then you best be eatin' quickly. If you finish up, I'll pay for a cab."

Jenna narrowed her eyes. And she thought her grandmother understood! She tore into her chicken leg like a wild animal. But then she couldn't swallow her first bite. She chewed and chewed and then swallowed some milk to go with it. Finally the chicken went down. She speared half the bowl of lettuce on her fork and stuffed that into her mouth. It was no use. She ended up spitting some out. Back to the chicken. She gagged on her second bite.

"My goodness, Girl Child. What's wrong with you. That's good chicken," Nana bellowed.

Loud, loud! Why was Nana making such a fuss? Jenna stared hard at her big flashy grandmother.

"Try some of that potato. Maybe that be goin' down easier," she suggested.

Jenna mashed up the potato with her fork and then brought some to her mouth. This time she downed it with milk immediately. "I'll never make it in time. Please, Nana. Don't make me! I'll be sick."

Her grandmother's face changed, crinkling into a thousand worry lines. "Can you get the milk down at least? You need something inside you," she said.

Jenna swallowed furiously. "Satisfied?" she asked.

Her grandmother frowned. "No, I am not satisfied. I'm thinkin' you're really not well enough to go dancin'."

Jenna jumped up, clenching her fists at her sides. "Please, just let me go! I'll be fine. Nana, I can't miss this rehearsal with Celine Laporte!"

☆CHAPTER SEVEN☆

Through the Camera's Eye

In the end, Nana called a cab. Jenna dashed into her room and slipped into her new white dance leotard. She had bought size small so it fit snugly. Jenna looked at herself in the mirror and thought she noticed a bulge in her stomach. Chicken, potato, milk, of course. What did she expect? She'd work if off tonight and maybe tomorrowwith an early morning jog.

"Just a little more weight to lose," she told herself in the mirror. "When this leotard fits loosely, the National Ballet costume should fit too." She threw on her sweats and then waited for her grandmother – the Food Enforcer.

Her gaze shifted to the books on her desk. Should she at least start on that French assignment? Mr Le Blanc was such a nag. Jenna had always done her homework on time and brilliantly. She'd expected a little more understanding from her teachers now that her life had turned into a big race to lose weight. It was hard to concentrate on anything when she always felt hungry. And with all the jogging she could never find time to remember, let alone sit down, and finish her school work.

"Taxi's here!" her grandmother called.

Jenna dashed down only half-realizing that her grandmother was rushing along beside her. "I can go by myself," she told her.

"Nonsense. You're not well and I'm not lettin' you go alone." Nana slammed the cab door and they were off.

The rehearsal took place at the Young People's Dance Theatre. They had supplied the other background dancers for Shawn Siamon's shoot. To Jenna's embarrassment, Nana insisted she would stay for the rehearsal as well.

Today she was wearing an emerald green two piece suit complete with huge green earrings that showed up like traffic lights because of her closely cropped hair. Her grandmother stood even taller than Jenna. Was Jenna doomed to grow that big? she wondered. Would she become as loud both in colour and tone? She frowned. It just didn't fit with her image of a ballet dancer.

In any case, there was no time to argue with Nana. Jenna rushed into the dingy dressing-room and stripped down to her leotard. She felt chilled so she put some leggings on over her tights.

When Jenna walked into the studio, she expected Matt to be hard at work at the *barre*. She didn't see him though. Her grandmother waved from the other end of the room and Jenna looked the other way. But it was no use. With mirrors on three walls, Nana waved to her from everywhere she looked. That's when Jenna noticed someone behind a large movie camera, standing on the opposite side, a bench away from her grandmother.

"Matt, what are you doing?" she called, shielding her eyes from the bright light at the top of his camera. "You have to rehearse too."

Matt didn't even look away from the viewfinder but he waved a hand. "That's perfect, stay right there for a moment. I'm just doing a white balance on your dance leotard."

"Matt Caruso! Answer me. Why aren't you at the *barre*?" She put her hands on her hips.

Matt's face appeared round the camera. "Because they don't need any male dancers." His tone sounded teasing and he smiled at her.

She didn't know why that made her so mad. She pulled a face at him.

"Come on, Jenna. I'm doing my English homework for a change." Then giving a sideways glance towards Jenna's grandmother, Matt stepped round the camera and closer to Jenna. He lowered his voice. "Which by the way, you haven't done. How come you didn't show up for the TV workshop again?"

Everything sank inside of Jenna. It was as though her brain was spinning out of control. How had she missed that again? Was she going out of her mind? But she couldn't admit that to Matt. "I...I'm just too busy for all that television nonsense," she blustered at him.

"You could have told me. I was worried." Matt's dark eyes weren't laughing and his lips were set in a straight line. He wasn't teasing or joking this time.

And she should have told him, he was right, which made Jenna uncomfortable. So she changed the subject. "Are you sure Celine Laporte will let you film her?"

"Video tape," Matt corrected her. "Yeah. Isn't it great? As long as I don't use the tape commercially, I can take all the footage I want."

"You'll have film of Celine Laporte dancing," Jenna said, suddenly envious.

"Hey," Matt said softly. "You know you'll be welcome to watch it any time you want." They were interrupted then as a short, grey-haired man walked into the room.

"Your attention, please," Jared Wesker, the instructor at Young People's Dance Theatre called. "If you could kindly interrupt your socializing to warm up please. I will tell you about the scene we will be performing as you stretch."

Jared Wesker folded his hands across his chest and frowned at Jenna. She curtsied quickly and then ran back to the *barre*. She launched into a *plié* as he spoke.

"We will be performing a piece from a theatre production of *The Red Shoes*, a Hans Christian Anderson fairy tale you may know. It's the story of a young girl who wears a pair of forbidden red shoes out of pride and vanity and is condemned to dance forever." Jared stopped. "And because you are working with me, you are condemned to rehearse forever! Andrea, straight back pul-lease."

Jared's steely grey eyes moved on to Jenna and she squirmed. "No chattering or slacking off. Hard work only or you're out! We begin."

Jared called out a string of dance moves in one long command. Then he snapped his fingers. "Come on, let's go. Over there, yes you, more elevation, please. Faster, faster." He clapped his hands to provide the tempo. "You must appear to be in a dancing frenzy. You can't stop! After this the young girl begs to have her legs chopped off, remember."

Jenna had always hated *The Red Shoes* fairy tale. Perhaps because of the bright colours her family always dressed in, wearing red shoes had never seemed such a great crime to her. Plus dancing forever hadn't seemed such a terrible fate even before she had fallen in love with ballet. But Jenna liked the wild quick number Jared Wesker had choreographed. The whirlwind pace and frenetic pace matched her mood.

"No smiles for this dance number," Jared coached. "Your expression should be desperate, frantic." He snapped his fingers at Jenna. "That's good. Exactly like her, everybody."

After half an hour of rehearsal, someone stepped into the room and Jared stopped everything. Jenna's mouth dropped open in awe. With the carriage of a queen, her ballet idol walked across the studio floor.

"Welcome, Miss Laporte." Jared raised an eyebrow and shot a pointed a look at the studio clock. "We were expecting you earlier." He frowned at the rest of the dancers as though it was their fault. "Take a ten minute break everyone to give Miss Laporte a chance to warm up."

Back behind the viewfinder, Matt shook his head in amazement. He'd never experienced dance in quite this way before. He'd panned in on the group, and focused on one dancer, Jenna, of course, and then even narrowed down his camera point of view to movements and certain parts of her body.

Did white really make people look heavier, Matt wondered, thinking over what Byron had said about the effects of colours. Would this optical weight gain show up through the viewfinder? He frowned. Jenna looked incredibly thin in spite of wearing a white dance leotard. He'd focused on her arms and shoulders to catch a *port de bras* on tape and noticed her neck first. He could see sinews like cords coming down from her head. When she'd turned, he'd been able to spot every bump of the vertebrae of her spine. Finally, when she raised her arms, he'd gasped. Her elbow joint appeared huge, at least twice as wide as her upper arm. If white added extra weight to a subject visually, then just how thin was Jenna? What he was seeing just couldn't be right or if it was, then Jenna couldn't possibly be healthy. He had to do something about it. Only what?

He felt a tap on his shoulder, and turned to face a statuesque woman dressed in vivid green. She grinned at him.

"You were talking to Jenna earlier," she

extended her hand to him. "I'm Beverley James, her grandmother."

Why hadn't Jenna introduced him to her? he wondered. She'd avoided her if anything. Matt sighed. On top of being too thin, Jenna was really prickly, and he didn't know how he could help her. He took Mrs James' hand and shook it. "I'm Matt Caruso. Pleased to meet you."

"Her dance partner?" She beamed at him.

"That's right."

"It's lovely to meet one of Jenna's friends," she confided. "I only see Jenna once a year and it's gettin' so hard to stay in touch with her, do you know?" The woman's brow furrowed, her eyes looked concerned.

Matt nodded. "She's a difficult person to know." Just in case that sounded like a criticism he quickly added, "But she's a very hard worker and an excellent dancer."

Mrs James clasped her hand round Matt's arm. "You don't say...? Tell me more about her."

☆CHAPTER EIGHT☆

Betrayal!

Matt spoke about all the things he thought his own grandmother would have liked to hear. He told Mrs James how Jenna had auditioned for William S. Holly and beat at least ten other dancers for her place. He explained how they'd worked together to choreograph their own dance number for the New York scholarship competition. He talked about busking with her in the park, how they'd done break dancing for people passing through, and how well she'd danced with the guest performers, The Tribal Beat. "Of course that's not Jenna's thing. Ballet is what she really wants to do."

Mrs. James smiled and nodded. She seemed to enjoy and agree with his anecdotes about Jenna. But then she looked him straight in the eye, cornering him. "Can you tell me why she thinks she needs to lose weight?"

Matt shifted from foot to foot. Could he tell her? What would Jenna think of him? He needed to stall. "Um, can I talk to you later?" He pointed to Celine Laporte coming out of the changing room.

"I'm just dying to videotape her. She's one of Jenna's heroines."

Mrs James' eyebrows lifted but her head nodded, understanding.

Matt trained the lens on Celine Laporte as she performed her *barre* warm-up exercises. Even though she was shorter than Jenna, her skin colour was exactly the same shade, a kind of warm caramel. Her exotic cheekbones also reminded Matt of Jenna and Jenna had a similar grace of movement.

The look on Celine's face was vacant, dreamy. She wore a smile fixed on her lips. As she moved, she seemed to conduct the music. Her exercises looked like a dance performance already. And when she executed a *port de bras*, Matt trained the camera on her shoulders and arms, the way he had for Jenna.

Interesting, he thought, as he saw the same kind of neck sinews protruding on her neck too. Every bone of her vertebrae poked out like Jenna's, and yes, her elbow joint appeared swollen in the middle of her toothpick arm. Celine looked just as sick as Jenna. Maybe it was just a female dancer thing, he thought, taking some comfort from that idea. Girls liked to be thin. His mother always seemed to be on some kind of diet. Maybe dancers just stayed thinner because of all the exercise. But the toothpick arms and swollen-looking elbow joints spooked him. No matter how he rationalized it, he still felt sick about what he'd seen through the camera.

When the group returned to the floor, and they practised the scene from *The Red Shoes*, Matt zoomed out from Celine Laporte to include the entire troupe. They danced faster and faster. He was sure he was getting something strong and powerful on his tape. Then he zoomed in on Jenna again and slowly panned across to Celine Laporte, zooming in on her, and then back to the group. Matt sensed something powerful, but was it *Dance is Everything* as Barry had suggested? Or *Dance is Life*? He wasn't sure.

"All right." Matt heard Mrs James' voice again as he unhooked the portable light from the top of the camera at the end of the rehearsal. "So we were talking earlier." He looked towards her. "Yes?"

"You were going to tell me why she thinks she needs to lose weight," Mrs James said.

He turned away again as he unscrewed the camera from the tripod. He didn't want to alarm Jenna's grandmother by telling her how he felt. "Jenna wants to dance classical ballet and it seems professional ballerinas are usually thin. I mean, look at Miss Laporte."

"The dancer who came in late?" Mrs James asked.

"Yes." Matt placed the camera gently back in the bag and zipped the case closed.

Mrs James clicked her tongue. "I don't know what the woman looks like normally but she's not lookin' too healthy today. And Jenna's gone crazy lately. She doesn't eat my Island cooking. It's too fattening, fine. But then I see her pickin' at her salad, too. And gaggin' on chicken. This can't be normal or right."

Matt frowned. "Well…it could be something that the assistant producer said when she was looking for dancers for the film last week…" Matt hesitated.

"Go on," Mrs James insisted, and Matt began to tell her about the costume size problem.

"Poor child." Mrs. James shook her head and clicked her tongue. "Maybe there's something her old grandma can do about that."

Next morning Jenna heard sizzling noises coming from the kitchen and a suffocating buttery smell assaulted her nose. Panicking, she leapt out of bed and rushed to the bathroom to step on the scales. She sighed with relief. Her weight had gone down. She felt encouraged, her resolve bolstered. Quickly she pulled on her jogging suit and slipped quietly out of the front door.

Her grandmother would force her to eat pancakes, she knew it, so she would try to run at least a mile first. Faster, faster, harder, harder — burn those calories, yes, yes, she thought as she ran. Round the first block, past the second, down the third, around and back home again. Then she tried to sneak back into her room.

"Girl Child, where in heaven's name did you go?" Nana asked. "Come and sit down. I made your favourite breakfast." Her grandmother waved a spatula at her.

"Pancakes were my favourite when I was six, Grandma." Jenna stepped into the kitchen, scowling at the plate sitting on the table, where, she realized, a large J-shaped pancake sat. She suddenly remembered the morning of that magical day when Nana took her to her *Giselle*. Nana had made her a J-shaped pancake then, too. Her heart melted for a moment and then seized up again. Another trick to fatten her up! "You made my initial. Oh Nana, I'm not a baby."

"No one's too old for a special breakfast now and again," her grandmother told her. But her voice didn't sound sure. She pulled out Jenna's chair for her. "You know, you shouldn't change yourself for anyone."

"What do you mean?" Jenna asked as she lowered herself into the chair.

"I know about the costume thing." She dropped her hand on Jenna's shoulder.

"What?" Jenna brushed it off. "Matt told you, didn't he? I can't believe it." She stood up again, feeling ready to kick something.

"Come on, Girl Child. You are a fabulous dancer. They should accept you as you are."

"What do you know? Sure, I can do African tribal dancing if I have a body like yours. For classical ballet, this is how I must be!" Hot tears of frustration ran down her cheeks.

"Jenna, sit down and eat your breakfast," her grandmother said softly.

"I can't!" Jenna wailed. "I have to shower and change."

"Eat your breakfast," she repeated just as softly, "or you aren't goin' anywhere."

At that point Jenna wanted to throw the plate at

her grandmother. Instead, tears running down her cheeks, she ate one J-shaped pancake with nothing on it. Then, still scowling at her grandmother, she pushed back her chair, got up and left.

☆CHAPTER NINE☆

The World Closes In

It was after nine that night when Matt returned the camera to Cablecity, but Byron Jennings was still sitting at his desk.

"Hey, you're back. Let's pop your tape into the editing suite and see what you have." Byron stood up and helped him put the camera, sun gun and tripod back in the storage room. Then Matt followed him into the control room. He fiddled with the dials and then stuck the videotape into a slot and pressed 'play'.

Byron sat with his arms folded across his chest. As they watched *The Red Shoes* dancers rehearse, he nodded. "You've got a great eye, Matt. And a good steady hand. What are you trying to say with this video?"

"*Dance is Life*?" Matt winced as he asked. "Remember we discussed it?"

"Yeah, I remember. But you keep focusing on these two dancers, and it makes the viewer start to compare them."

Matt blushed. "One's a friend and the other is Celine Laporte."

"They have similar styles, don't they? Or do they just look the same?" He shrugged his shoulders. "I'm no dance expert, but the viewer will compare them. That's OK but you should use it within your story." Byron pushed the rewind button and played the shots again. "Look at their eyes. They're the same."

Matt squinted at the small television screen in front of him. "What are you talking about? Jenna's are brown and Celine's are green."

"Not colour, Matt. Look at the expression in them." He stopped the frame with Jenna in it for a moment and then the next frame with Celine in it.

Matt expected to see steely determination in their eyes. But instead, he saw something else. Dreaminess? They were in some other worlds of their own. He shuddered. Dreamy was too comforting a word. Their eyes looked vacant, as though possessed.

"Is that what dance is all about? Can we see it by the expression in their eyes?" Byron turned to look at him.

Matt shrugged his shoulders.

"Well, something to think about, anyway." Byron rewound the tape. "We can just cut some of the shots if you don't want to say anything with them. Sometimes the videotape editor creates the whole story by just keeping the good ones. You're reserving the camera again, right?" he asked as he handed Matt his videotape back.

"Is tomorrow too soon?" Matt asked. "I wanted

to get some school dancing on my tape."

"Mmm," Byron said. "Let's go back and check. I think I saw someone's name on the clipboard."

The name turned out to be Daniel Reeve which was perfect, Matt thought. He'd call Dan and ask him to film his and Jenna's scholarship dance at lunchtime.

Next morning, a huge old car complete with tail fins and bullet point fenders, came rattling into the car park. Matt grinned as a middle-aged man in white tights, strange shoes and a short white pleated skirt stepped out. "Still writing the Greek book, Mr Reeve?"

"Eees coming along, nicely. Chaptair ten now." Mr Reeve said in a thick accent. He helped load Dan up with the camera bag and tripod. "Good luck with the feelming," he told them as he slid back into the car.

"Videotaping," Dan corrected him under his breath. Then he held up his hand to Matt. "Don't say a word! He told me he wouldn't go this far but then he developed writer's block. The costumes help him, what can I say?" Dan shrugged helplessly. Then he shook his head. "Honestly, Matt, I think my father's really going off the deep end on this Greek book."

Matt thumped him on the back. "Well, but at least he's got your great legs!"

The two of them strolled into the school together and down the hall, with Matt protecting Dan's camera side from the students who were pushing past in the morning rush hour.

Suddenly, Jenna hurled herself at Matt from out of nowhere. She grabbed fistfuls of his T-shirt. "I can't believe you, Matt Caruso! You told my grandmother about me dieting to fit the National Ballet costume?"

Matt could feel her knuckles digging into his chest. He covered her hands with his. She looked so wild – hysterical really. "Calm down, Jenna." He removed her hands from his T-shirt, still holding them as he brought them down. "Your grandmother's a cool lady. We got to talking and then she kept asking about why you wanted to diet."

"Why did you have to tell her?" she hissed at him, her eyes sparking in anger.

"I didn't mean to," he said. "You know me, I'm a blabbermouth, I'm sorry." She still looked furious, like a pot boiling over. "Did you get into a lot of trouble?"

"My grandmother made me eat a pancake," she said and then strode away without a backward glance.

"No! Anything but that!" Dan joked.

"It's not funny," Matt told him. "I'm beginning to think there's something really wrong with Jenna."

"She's always been wound up too tightly, if you ask me." Dan patted him on the shoulder. "You were just too much in love to see it."

"Maybe," Matt smiled, wanting so much to believe Dan. Then he punched him back. "Hey, I'm *still* in love."

"So am I." Dan was smiling as he saw Nikki

coming towards him, a rolled-up drawing under her arm.

Jenna still felt too angry to sit with the gang at lunch-time, even if there was a seat free. All those crowds of art students! She was sick of them watching her eat, spying really! They had no self control. It was sickening the way they shovelled greasy hamburgers and french fries into themselves. Didn't they know about the fat content? Didn't they care? Instead, Jenna found herself a seat in the dance studio where the warm air blew up from a heating vent. Why was it so cold everywhere, she wondered as she sucked on a tiny wedge of celery.

Miss Adaman walked in a few moments later spoiling Jenna's chance of being away from prying eyes.

"Hi, Jenna!" She placed her tray on the piano and took an egg salad sandwich from the plate.

Jenna could smell the sweet mayonnaise, the tangy bits of onion, the bitter strength of her coffee. And something else. On top of all that, the smell of a warm sugary cinnamon bun.

Miss Adaman bit into her sandwich, licking a bit of egg from her lip. "You're early today. Where's Matt?" She chewed silently as she waited for an answer.

"I don't know." The words came out sounding churlish. Jenna finished her last bit of celery, then shut and put away the container.

"Was that all you had? Or did you forget your lunch? I bought this cinnamon bun because it looked so good and I'm never going to eat it all," she said, holding it out to Jenna.

"No," Jenna snapped.

Miss Adaman went on eating her sandwich – chewing, chewing. Finally she asked. "No, you didn't forget your lunch or no, you didn't want the cinnamon bun? I really don't need all the extra fat," she coaxed. "You're welcome to it." Miss Adaman held out the bun again by the waxy paper that stuck to the white icing.

"No to both," Jenna said firmly. What was it with everybody? She'd thought it was just Nana, but now they all wanted her to eat their high fat food.

Miss Adaman tilted her head to one side. "Is there something bothering you?"

Jenna bit the inside of her cheeks till she tasted something salty. "You thought I would love The Tribal Beat. Me especially."

"Ahh!" Miss Adaman shook her head. "It's because you have such tunnel vision where dance is concerned. Classical ballet seems to be all you want to know. But Jenna..." she paused.

"Yes?" Jenna fidgeted with one of her braids avoiding Miss Adaman's eyes.

"...dance evolves with every generation. We study character dancing because some ballet scenes need them, but we also take it to add bits of other culture to our dances. That's what makes dance a living, breathing art form."

At that moment, Matt walked into the studio looking as though he was ducking flying objects.

"Is it all right, Miss Adaman, if Dan videotapes Jenna and me doing our New York dance? It's for my English project. And he only has the camera for one day."

Miss Adaman nodded.

"Jenna?" he asked.

She wanted him to stop all this television production nonsense. It was distracting him from dance. She narrowed her eyes at him but in the end with Miss Adaman watching, she felt she had to agree.

"Go ahead, video the dance," Jenna grumbled.

"Great, thanks!"

They warmed up as usual and then Matt stuck the tape with their music into the player. Jenna led the dance in the beginning. It was a follow-the-leader movement inspired by their old game of leaping over parking meters. She loved the fun and freedom of it, felt her heart leaping over the hurdles in her life.

Then the dance moved into expressions of Matt and Jenna's problems. Matt danced as though he was trapped in a low-ceilinged room. Jenna danced as though she was a model posing in tight constraining clothing. That tightness clutched at her like a size small ballet tutu. Matt hoisted her like a sack of vegetables, parodying a bad ballet lift. *This is why I must lose weight*, she thought.

Then they both burst through the walls of their life, reaching for something higher and better.

Jenna usually felt great when they'd finished this dance. It was as though, when they danced through those imaginary walls, she could conquer everything. She usually ended with an exhilarating feeling of hope.

Only not today. Today the hurdles seemed too high, the clothing too tight. She thought she'd never be light enough for Matt or classical ballet.

Miss Adaman smiled as they bowed. "Don't you see, Jenna? Your world is so much wider than classical ballet."

☆CHAPTER TEN☆

The Lie

There had been three horrible rehearsals for *The Red Shoes* number in Shawn Siamon's film. Horrible, because Jared Wesker browbeat them into a frenzy of dance. It wasn't real ballet at all. Awful too because Celiné Laporte never danced with them again. "The great prima ballerina will join us again for the last rehearsal," Jared had told them simply.

Jenna's whole being seemed to be centred on her stomach these days. During the rehearsal sessions, her mouth tasted bad – acidic – and she felt exactly the way it tasted. When she finished that evening, the last thing she needed was to be nagged by Matt.

"Jenna, I'd like to visit The Tribal Beat open workshop this Sunday. Wanna come?" he asked eagerly.

"Why? Because I'm black?" she snapped.

"What? Jenna, this is me, Matt! I'm going because I'd like to do some videotaping of their dances. I asked you because you're the only dance friend I have."

If her nerves weren't sparking and snapping inside her, she might have seen straight enough to apologize. Instead she became defensive and huffy. "Why are you even here filming again? When are you going to finish with your stupid movie? You're supposed to be a dancer, Matt!" Then something inside her did snap and she suddenly felt loose and swirly, light and floating, and then, just as suddenly, dark and heavy. She sank into a black hole.

"Jenna, Jenna!" Matt called to her as if from far away. Jenna forced her eyes open and tried to focus on his blurry figure. He held a glass of water out to her. "You fainted. Have a sip, come on."

Jenna blinked a few times and sat up. Finally her vision cleared and she took the glass from Matt's hand, gulping the water down.

"Maybe your blood sugar's low. Let me get you an apple. I've got some fruit in the camera bag." He reached into one of the side pockets and pulled out a green apple.

"Thanks," Jenna whispered submissively. She took a bite and then chewed it for a long time. Another and then another. Finally, Matt helped her up.

Jenna brushed off her tights. "I have to get going. Mum will be here to pick me up any minute." She started walking to the changing room.

"Jenna?" Matt called.

She stopped and turned. "What?"

"Do you think you should see a doctor?" he asked softly. "About the fainting."

"No, I can't! I don't have the time right now. Besides, doctors don't understand anything about dancing."

Matt's eyes narrowed. To Jenna, he looked suspicious and prying like all the others.

"Honestly, it's this crazy wild dancing, Matt. I just need to get through Shawn Siamon's movie shoot." She took his shoulders in her hands and squeezed them, trying to force him to believe her. "After that, I'll catch up on my homework, I'll be able to relax again. I'll even eat a chocolate bar with you. It'll be great." As she said it, she felt her nerves uncurl and she smiled at Matt because, even if *he* couldn't believe her anymore, she truly believed every word she had told him.

"You're on, Jenna. Only I don't want to eat just a chocolate bar. I want to share a pizza with you somewhere away from this place, for once."

They walked outside towards the car park and Jenna's mum offered Matt a lift.

"No thanks. My mum's picking me up too. We have to return the camera to Cablecity." He waved at Jenna as they pulled away.

"He's a nice boy," Jenna's mother told her. "Is he over his glandular fever now? Will he be well enough to go to that New York dance workshop?"

Jenna tossed her braids back. "Oh, he's fine! I just hope he can keep his concentration on dance instead of film making."

"Jenna…" her mother paused.

Jenna didn't like the tone. It was her we-have-to-have-a-serious-talk tone. "What?" she said, staring out the window, hoping her lack of interest would put off her mother.

"Your grandmother's only going to be here another couple of weeks. And if you're not out jogging, you barricade yourself in your room. You haven't been around very much. She thinks you're avoiding her."

"I go to school all day, I have ballet practice...television production, homework..." Jenna lied and floundered to cover up the fact that she had been avoiding Nana the Food Enforcer. "Besides," she finished, "She doesn't like me."

"Don't be foolish. Now your daddy's dead, you and Joyce are all she has left of him." Her mother sighed. "She's gone to a great deal of trouble to arrange a special surprise for you. And I really want you to understand and be grateful."

Jenna turned to look at her mother. "What? More food?"

"No! It's something to do with ballet, of course."

Ballet tickets – Jenna instantly knew and despite herself, felt warm and loved again. Especially by Nana. Perhaps tickets to *Swan Lake*, the National Ballet was performing it this month. Jenna's lips lifted into a smile. She could forgive all the loudness and brightness of Grandma if she took her to *Swan Lake*. Jenna hugged herself with joy.

When the car stopped in the garage space, Jenna raced to the elevator to hit the 'up' button. When the doors slid open, she called to her mother. "Hurry!"

"Now, don't you let on I told you anything. And

no matter what, I want you to be grateful, understand?" Up the elevator, down the corridor to their door, and finally her mother twisted her key in the lock. Jenna rushed through the door.

Her grandmother was sitting in the living room, smiling at her. She didn't say a word but her eyes glanced over to the curtain where a dress hung from the rod.

Jenna stared at it. It was white and gauzy – long and old-fashioned. A little red vest hung over top of the shoulders. A flash of red from the floor distracted her. Red shoes, she realized. Red ballet shoes.

"It's the costume you'll be needin' for that ballet in your movie," Nana explained.

"What? But how did you get it? And why?"

"My old friend doesn't work at the National Ballet any more but she helped me pull a few strings. The wardrobe mistress found this costume. It's a size medium, honey, your size. You don't have to be dietin' any more." Her grandmother beamed at her.

Jenna's hands flew to her face and she squeezed her head as though in pain. "But I don't wear the red shoes! Celine Laporte is the principal dancer."

"I know that too, Girl Child. They don't loan shoes. I bought them for you special. Somethin' extra to brighten you up a little when you're dancin' just for yourself." She picked them up and held them out to Jenna. "Try them on. They are so nice." She lovingly stroked the tops with her thumb .

Jenna backed away. "Red shoes? No. And

Grandma, I don't wear size medium anymore. Ballet dancers can't be that big!"

"Rubbish! You are one heck of a dancer, Girl Child, and if you be extra jumbo size, I say they be sewin' you an extra jumbo size tutu. You don't starve yourself for nobody."

"Don't you understand? I just can't be like you and Mum and Joyce. I don't want to be bright and big. I just can't!" Jenna shook her head and ran off to her bedroom.

She flung herself across her bed but didn't even feel like crying. Instead everything inside her raced. She felt cold and light-headed and jittery, really jittery. She jumped up to find her jogging things just as her mother pushed open the door.

"Now you listen to me, young lady. You can be serious as the hot sun about ballet, but that doesn't mean you can treat everyone you love like they're your dance floor." She shook her finger at Jenna. "I want you to think about what your grandmother did for you and I want you to come out and thank her. Or stay in here till you do!" Her mother turned on her heels and slammed the door behind her.

Jenna sat down on her bed. They all wanted so much from her. It was hard to know what to do next and her whole body twitched and jumped. She couldn't keep her knees still as she sat, so she jumped up and paced around the room. No good. She needed to get out of there. She needed to run. To pound the pavement hard. That was it. She put on her tracksuit and headed for the living room.

She forced herself to smile. "Nana, I'm sorry. It's

just..." she lowered her voice a little to deliver the lie, "...I have a bad headache and I'm not myself. I'm going on a little run to clear it. Then I'll be right back to try on those red shoes."

☆CHAPTER ELEVEN☆

True Friends

"She never eats with us any more. I'm not sure she eats at all. I'm really worried," Matt told the others around the canteen table at lunch-time.

"Well, she nibbles some lettuce and stuff in the dance studio, doesn't she?" Abbi asked.

"Oh right," Lauren said. "Then how come, when I left at lunch for a dentist appointment, I spotted her running outside."

Abbi shook her head. "I just can't believe Jenna's changed so much. She once told *me* off about missing a meal, accused me of being anorexic."

Nikki looked up from her unhappy doodling. "It's that bad, isn't it? I mean you really think she is..."

Dan scratched at his head. For once even he didn't have a joke. "How long can she go on like this?"

"Who knows," Matt winced. "She's gone ballistic over this movie shoot. But she promised when it's done she'll even eat chocolate."

"When's the shoot?" Abbi asked.

"The last rehearsal is Monday. Celine Laporte's going to be there again. Then they're shooting on Tuesday. I just wish I was sure she'd snap out of it after that. I don't want to rat on her again like I did about the costume. She'll never forgive me."

"I say you should give her the chance," Nikki said. "Once the shoot's over you must go to Miss Adaman, Mr Flieder, her mother, her sister..."

Her grandmother, Matt thought.

"...anyone who will get her some help," Nikki continued. "That's if she doesn't start eating again."

Matt chewed his lip. He had such a bad feeling. Her strange behaviour had gone on for so long, since December, really, but he had ignored it till the costume crisis. What were the chances that she would go back to her old self when the movie was done? Meanwhile, could he just wait and watch as she starved herself to death? He got up from the table. "I'm going to go and find Jenna and talk to her myself."

He looked for her in the dance studio – but found no Jenna there. He searched the halls and the library and then headed outside, just in time to see her jogging towards the school gate.

"Jenna!" He waved. Was it his imagination or did she frown? He ran over to meet her. "We missed you at lunch. You ready to practise?"

Jenna panted but nodded when she caught her breath.

"Here, have an apple. I know you didn't have time to eat." He tossed her the polished red fruit and this time he really did see her pull a face.

"Don't worry, I have one for myself. Benefits of owning a store." He bit into another red apple.

"Maybe, after practice," Jenna said, tucking the apple into her jacket pocket.

He decided right then that he wouldn't let her do that to herself. "I'm eating mine now so you'll have to wait for me anyway."

"But I want to clean up before dancing..."

She's arguing this much about a piece of fruit, he thought. He couldn't let it go on any longer. "I'm not having you faint on me again. Eat it while we walk or I won't practise with you."

"Fine," she snapped and crunched angrily into the apple.

"It's good isn't it? No fat, lots of fibre, a little bit of fructose for energy." He felt proud of the last detail. It would have impressed the old Jenna.

The new one continued to chew resentfully as she strode towards the studio.

As he struggled to keep up with her, Matt promised himself that he would protect Jenna as best he could even if it were only from herself. He would spend as much time with her as possible, make sure she didn't totally starve, try to kid her out of this thing. "Last rehearsal on Monday, you must be excited. Then it will all be over." And if it wasn't, he said to himself, he would call in outside help.

Jenna finally broke the silence. "I would be excited but I just don't get the scene. I don't know how the characters feel, how they can be unhappy to dance. We're not supposed to smile. We're supposed to dance in a daze." She threw up her hands.

"You know the library has the video of the 1947 Hollywood production of *The Red Shoes*. I'm borrowing it to study at home. I needed some ideas for my own video..." when Matt saw Jenna's lip curl, he quickly substituted "...English project."

"I wish I could see it," Jenna said.

"Come on over after school." He couldn't believe she was playing right into his hands. "You can eat supper with us." They were at the studio door now. He turned the handle.

"No, no, that's OK. I need to spend time with my grandma. I'll come over later." She followed him into the room.

After they'd warmed up, they went through the New York routine as usual. It was odd how different Jenna felt towards the dance. Jogging to burn off calories took so much time, somehow she always felt as though she was running through the rest of her life to catch up. Pressure and more pressure. Her movements reflected her feelings. The follow-the-leader routine seemed somehow now to be a chase, the dances showing Matt and Jenna trapped in their own worlds seemed more intense. When Jenna burst from the walls of her world, it seemed a more desperate escape. Everything was urgent, like their last dance on earth. Dancing in a daze, Jenna had called her *Red Shoes* rehearsals. But now that was what their New York piece felt like too.

When they finished, they towelled down before

their regular dance class. Matt wondered how Jenna could keep it up. First jogging, then rehearsal, then more dance – and all on five bites of apple.

The rest of the afternoon Matt invited their other friends to come to his house for the film. "Come on. It'll be fun," he told Dan and Nikki.

"Fun?" Dan raised an eyebrow.

"I don't really understand ballet," Nikki offered apologetically.

"*The Red Shoes* won the Academy Award for Best Art Direction. That might interest you," Matt growled. "All right. I'll admit it. I can't face Jenna alone anymore. I'm afraid I'll just end up yelling at her or shaking her and then losing her totally," Matt said in a halting voice.

Dan pursed his lips. "We'll be there."

Nikki nodded. "I'll bring some snacks."

Abbi and Lauren agreed too, when he bumped into them.

"You are a really good friend," Lauren said softly, touching Matt's shoulders.

He smiled sadly. "That's what Jenna needs right now."

☆CHAPTER TWELVE☆

The Red Shoes

The smell of nutmeg clung to everything in Jenna's apartment. It was a Grenadian smell, Joyce told her, when she complained. But still over it all, Jenna smelled something even stronger. Supper?

"Special Island beef patties," Grandma told her.

"Oh, I'm invited to Matt's house for dinner," she said, even though she had no intention of eating there either.

"In my day it wasn't proper, a girl goin' to visit a boy like that." Her grandmother clicked her tongue. Then she softened. "But he's a nice boy." She sighed. "And Lord knows, it's not my day any more."

"Oh sure it is!" Joyce, the good sister, ran over and gave her grandmother a big hug.

Jenna shifted from foot to foot uncomfortably. The last hug she'd given Nana was at the airport. But that had been before she'd announced her campaign to fatten Jenna up. Fighting Nana about food all the time sucked the energy and affection for her grandmother right out of Jenna. "Well, I'll just finish a bit of homework and then I'm going round to Matt's to watch *The Red Shoes*."

"You want a lift?" Joyce asked, breaking apart from Grandma. "I've got Mum's car."

"No, I like to walk." Jenna dashed into her room and threw her tracksuit on. It was really her favourite outfit lately. Big and warm and comfy. She looked at the stack of school books on her desk and hesitated. Then she grabbed a jacket and headed for the door.

It took an hour to walk to Matt's usually, but Jenna covered the distance in thirty-five minutes. Her stride was long and hard and determined.

Her only hope was that she didn't arrive in the middle of Matt's dinner. Mrs Caruso would probably insist she sit in on one of their heavy Italian meals. She hesitated outside his house but then a little red car pulled up.

"Hey!" Abbi's voice called.

"You're coming to see *The Red Shoes*?" Jenna asked, turning her head to one side.

"Oh yeah. It's a classic. Nominated for five Academy Awards, won two." Abbi smiled as she caught up with Jenna.

Another car rolled to the curb and Lauren hopped out.

"Don't tell me you're interested in ballet?" Jenna asked her.

"Of course," Lauren answered. "Besides, *The Red Shoes* won Best Music Score."

The three strolled up the walkway together and rang the bell. Dan let them in. "You're here, too?" Jenna commented.

"And Nikki. Come on in, we're just watching the tail end of *Goldfinger*. Anyone for pizza?"

"Sure," Abbi answered for all of them and they followed Dan down the stairs to Matt's part of the house.

"Hi, Jenna," Matt called. On the television screen James Bond curled up with his latest girlfriend in a life raft. "Abbi, Lauren, take a seat. Grab some pizza. The snacks are over there." He didn't say anything about the fruit bowl in the middle of the coffee table. Kiwis, grapes, strawberries and bananas were heaped around pears and apples. "Could you just rewind *Goldfinger* for me Nikki?"

Nikki pressed a button on the remote control.

Matt turned to Jenna now, smiling and trying to sound casual. "Do you think you could help with my English project? I need more variety in my dance video and you're my main character. Could you come to The Tribal Beat workshop with me?"

Jenna shook her braids.

"Please. I'll get thrown out of William Holly if I don't get a higher English mark."

With all their friends surrounding them, she felt as though Matt was trapping her, forcing her to go.

"Besides, tribal dancing will burn just as many calories as all that jogging you're doing." Matt gave her a sharp look.

Finally, Jenna had to agree. "As long as it's not Monday or Tuesday night."

"Nah, it's Sunday afternoon. Don't you remember?" Matt asked. "Right, *The Red Shoes* video. Dan, would you put it in for me?"

"And *play*," Nikki said as she pressed a button on the remote control.

It opened with a group of friends at a theatre watching a ballet.

"Look at the size of that girl's thighs!" Dan commented as a dancer whirled across the stage. "I mean, I know you guys get big muscles from dancing, but wow!"

"Her arms are fat," Jenna said flatly.

"Fat?" Lauren said. "Rounded maybe. Ballet dancers certainly were rounder back in 1947."

"They're huge!" Dan sputtered. "It's amazing."

"Shh!" Abbi told them. "We want to hear the story."

Jenna enjoyed the film in spite of herself. The main character was Victoria Page, a wealthy girl who also happened to be fabulous at ballet. The ballet company director, Boris Lermontov, seemed as mean as Mr Rudolph and the dance coach, behaved a lot like Jared Wesker.

As Victoria rose in fame she fell in love with the composer, Julian Craster, only Boris Lermontov fired him from the ballet the moment he discovered they were in love. Dance was supposed to be everything. She couldn't have it both ways, Boris told Victoria. But Victoria ran away and married Julian. At the opening performance of her husband's new opera, she was lured back to dance her role in *The Red Shoes* – Boris Lermontov's new show. Julian feigned illness to chase after her and just before the curtain went up, he and Boris pulled and pushed at Victoria to make her choose between them. Julian left in dismay. Victoria became so distraught, instead of running out on to the stage to dance, she leapt out of the window and was hit by a car.

The best part of the movie for Jenna was when Boris announced to the audience that Victoria would never dance again, but that the ballet would go on that evening because it's what she would have wanted. But the whole ballet was performed with only a white spotlight where Victoria should have been dancing.

Jenna sighed at the end. Victoria had looked so lovely as she lay dying – just a few bruises and not fat like the other dancers. Dying while you were still young and beautiful seemed like such a romantic way to go.

☆ CHAPTER THIRTEEN ☆

Too Far Gone

"Do you think I could splice a few dancing scenes from the old version of *The Red Shoes* into my videotape?" Matt asked as Dan helped him set up a Cablecity camera in The Tribal Beat's dance studio.

"Are you kidding? With the editing suite at Cablecity?" Dan waved his hand as though whisking away all doubts. "It shouldn't be any problem."

"It would be so neat to contrast it with the stuff I'm taping now." Matt panned the camera around the room. All shapes and sizes of people limbered up and stretched, warming up for the workshop. And they weren't only black, as Jenna had thought. Asians, Caucasians, it didn't matter, they all just seemed to be laughing and chatting as they prepared to have a good time.

"Jenna's here now," Dan said as she came out of the changing room. "Why does she always wear those awful sweats? Look at them, they hang on her."

"You'd think she'd be too hot." Matt took his head away from the viewfinder for just a moment to strip off his own sweater. "Phew, that's better," he said, and tugged at the shoulders of his white T-shirt to loosen it from his body.

When he peered back through the lens, he recognized the guest performers who had visited Holly. They had gathered near the front of the studio.

"People!" Jamal called as he stepped into the centre of the floor. Miguel, Ellen, Kayla and Margaret lined up beside him. "We want to introduce you to step dancing this afternoon." As he spoke his feet started to pound the floor in a slow rhythm. "It's a form of modern dancing that hails from South Africa. Join in." Miguel, Ellen, Kayla and Margaret's feet now began to beat the same rhythm into the floor.

Matt felt the vibrations through the camera – heavy and slow.

Next, Jamel clapped twice so that the pattern became stomp, stomp, clap-clap, stomp, stomp, clap-clap.

Then the other four joined in. Jamel motioned with his hand for Jenna and the others in the room to try. Jenna stepped lightly and then clapped.

"No, no. Not on the balls of your feet. That's too light," he advised. "This is a heavy foot movement. Flatten your feet."

Jenna stamped a bit harder now.

"Bend your knees just a little. It will give you more power. Don't lift from your rib cage. This is not ballet. It's not up, up, up!" Jamel instructed. "It's down, down, down." He crouched a little to exaggerate the movement. "You got it!" he suddenly called. "Get into it!" Stomp, stomp, clap-clap. "Six times and then we'll do a single stomp and change from the clap-clap to a slap-slap on the hips." Jamal demonstrated as the others all followed. "You got it! Now get into it!"

The whole room stamped. The whole room clapped. Matt could stand it no longer. His whole body itched to take on the beat. "You take over," he told Dan, unbuckling the lighting belt and putting it round Dan. Dan stepped into his place by the camera and Matt ran on to the dance floor. Stomp, stomp, slap-slap.

"Smile, loosen up!" Jamel called towards Jenna.

Jenna's full toothed smile looked more like an angry grimace.

Matt found a place beside her, raised his eyebrows in a challenge and then stomped heavier than an elephant. He clapped as hard as he could, too, and of course Jenna reacted. Her stomp became thunderous, her clap turned into a whip crack.

"OK. Let's change from the clap to the hip slap," Jamal told them. "On the end of this phrase… Ready, one, two, slap-slap."

It sounded softer but the vibrations and heavy beat seemed to have taken Jenna over already. She looked happy as she tried to compete with Matt. Always has to be the best, he thought, smiling to himself.

"Admit it. You had fun, Jenna," Matt teased her after the session when they met back in the hall.

"Of course! But serious dance isn't about fun.

It's about passion. Putting everything into the art. Eating and breathing ballet," she told him.

Almost normal, he thought, as Dan rolled his eyes at him when Jenna wasn't looking. At least Jenna going nuts about ballet was more normal than her going paranoid about food. "I brought some drinks and some fruit in my bag," he gestured with his head.

"Diet drinks?" Her paranoia snapped back into place again.

"You don't want that stuff. It has artificial sweetener. I brought orange and pineapple juice. Which do you want? Dan?"

"An ice cream sundae, thank you very much. I'm meeting Nikki at Hamburger Palace. See you guys." He handed the camera bag back to Matt and left the building.

"Here," Matt handed Jenna the pineapple juice. "It's got less calories than the orange juice. Jenna, there's something I need to talk to you about. I wanted to wait till after Shawn Siamon's shoot of the ballet scene but I don't think it's a good idea to wait anymore...I'm worried about you, Jenna."

Jenna froze mentally when anyone took that tone with her. Everyone was *concerned*, that's how the talks always began. She wasn't eating enough to stay healthy, that's how they continued. Grandma especially never let up. She had to start eating more, that's how all of them ended. The whole world wanted to trick her into losing her only chance at ballet. They all wanted her to be fat. She avoided Nana now, couldn't wait for her to set out on her flight next week.

"...and I want you to get help," Matt was lecturing her and she didn't want to listen. "See a counsellor at school. Or I have this number for a teenagers' advice hot line..."

Jenna switched back in on his words. This sounded different, this sounded *worse*. "What! You're supposed to understand! You're my friend! But you know...you're just like all the rest."

"Jenna, I'm scared for you. You're not just dieting. It's gone too far."

She cut him off. "I know what I'm doing."

He shook his head.

"I just have to be thin for ballet!" She yelled at him in frustration, then turned on her heels and ran from the building.

Happily, the bus pulled up to the stop right away so that Matt couldn't catch up with her. When Jenna arrived back home, she didn't pick up the telephone as it rang and rang and rang.

Tomorrow was the rehearsal. Celine Laporte would be there. Everything would be perfect then. Celine was thin and she was black. Maybe Jenna could talk to her and she could give her tips on how to handle all these difficult people around her. They could share a laugh, go jogging sometime. Maybe Celine would even ask her to join the ballet corps. Jenna was probably hoping for too much from Celine but as she wiped the tears from her cheeks, Jenna needed to promise herself something...that tomorrow things would be great. Tomorrow things would be perfect.

☆CHAPTER FOURTEEN☆

The Empty Spotlight

The last rehearsal was in full costume. Jenna brought the medium size dress her grandmother had borrowed from the National Ballet. She would show that wardrobe mistress. Her body swam in the medium size dress since Jenna had toughened up on her diet. She had to wear size small now.

Joyce drove her to the Young People's Dance Theatre. "I hope you make your peace with Nana before she goes, Jenna. Who knows when we're going to see her again. And she's getting old..."

Jenna gripped the handle of her duffle bag so tightly her knuckles turned white. "Please, Joyce, I really need to focus on my performance right now."

Joyce screwed up her mouth but said nothing more on the subject. Ten minutes later, she pulled the car up to the front of the theatre. "Call me when you're through and I'll pick you up," she told Jenna. "See you then."

Jenna slammed the car door and Joyce drove away.

Up the stairs, into the change room, Jenna couldn't believe how nervous she felt. Everything raced inside her. It was as though her heart was bouncing on a tambourine.

The wardrobe mistress stood at attention near a rack of costumes against the wall and Jenna handed her the dress. "My grandmother borrowed this from you. Her name is Mrs Beverley James."

"You can wear it if you like. Mr Siamon already told me he wanted you to dance."

A little thrill raced through her. Shawn Siamon wanted her to dance! Then she tossed her braids proudly. "I wear a size small now." She waited for a comment from the woman. – What willpower! Good for you! Anything like that. Instead she just exchanged costumes with Jenna. She could stand to lose some weight, Jenna thought. She was probably just jealous.

Jenna changed into the costume immediately. It felt perfect. Then she went out to do her warm-ups at the *barre*. There was Matt again, with his annoying camera and bright light. She refused to look at him as she did a *plié* but she couldn't help seeing him in the mirrors, always spying on her through that lens.

The other dancers drifted in and Jenna found herself searching hopefully for Celine Laporte. Perhaps she changed somewhere else? Certainly she would make a grand entrance, Jenna thought. She wouldn't have to look for her.

Then Jared Wesker strutted in, eyeing them all with a frown.

"Concentration pul-lease. Stop chattering like a bunch of monkeys."

Jenna hadn't heard anyone talking at all. Wesker continued marching alongside the dancers at the *barre*. "Elevation, come on. Straight arm. Lift from the ribcage." He touched her foot, correcting a movement. Back and forth.

The piano player began the music from *The Red Shoes* number and Jared Wesker looked up at the clock, clicking his tongue. "All right, we rehearse without the great and wonderful prima ballerina, again," he said, tossing his hand as though dismissing her.

It was only a short number with the chorus dancers providing a foil for Celine Laporte's dancing. They pirouetted in a frenzy just as they had rehearsed. It didn't look like the beautiful graceful kind of ballet Jenna loved but it had a kind of energy, like the hall at school when the morning bell rang. When Shawn Siamon walked into the studio, Jenna was relieved to be able to rest.

"Really, Mr Siamon," Jared Wesker addressed him, flicking his head disdainfully. "I take your word for it that Miss Laporte is a great, great dancer because I so seldom see her. Is she even going to present herself for the filming?"

Shawn Siamon shook his head and the look on his face stopped Jared Wesker's sarcastic tirade. The movie producer walked to the front of the studio and raised his hands. He didn't have the same presence as Celine Laporte, he simply didn't have the grace or sparkle. But even in the brown casual clothing he wore as a uniform, he did convey a quiet kind of assurance when he spoke to people. Perhaps his years as a Holly student had given him that.

He didn't speak for a moment. Instead, he took off his glasses and wiped them. He cleared his throat, frowned hard as though fighting something, looked up to the ceiling and then out towards the dancers again. "I'm not sure how to give you this news. This is a terrible shock for all of us…" He stopped and swallowed hard and then began again. "Earlier this evening, Miss Celine Laporte was rushed to hospital after suffering from cardiac arrest."

Jenna's own heart felt as though it had stopped at that moment. "No!" someone gasped. It was what Jenna would have said if she weren't frozen in disbelief.

"Some of you may know that Miss Laporte was on sick leave from the National Ballet. She was fighting a long battle with an eating disorder, but we all felt that she was winning. Unfortunately, her heart has been seriously weakened by her struggles." Shawn Siamon paused, looking at the ceiling again. "Celine Laporte," he looked back to the students, "is resting in intensive care right now. But she is listed as critical. Please give her your thoughts and prayers."

Jenna felt her own legs buckle at the same time as she felt strong arms support her.

"It's OK, Jenna," Matt's voice spoke to her gently through the haze. "I'm here. It's going to be all right."

She heard herself crying then, tasted salty wet

tears, clutched at Matt desperately; yet through it all Jenna felt as though it was a different person who was behaving like that, a small weak version of herself.

"My mum's waiting right outside. I'm going to take you to the car. We'll get your stuff later."

Jenna nodded mutely.

The two of them struggled out of the door, Jenna leaning on Matt. "Jenna's not feeling well, Mum. We just heard Celine Laporte had a heart attack and may be dying."

His mother nodded and they drove off immediately.

Matt continued to hold Jenna. "I know you're really upset, we all are. But when we get home, I have something I have to show you. Something that can't wait any longer."

☆CHAPTER FIFTEEN☆

New Possibilities

Jenna sat on the couch shivering beneath a crocheted blanket.

"Drink your tea, you'll get warmer." Matt was fiddling with the television set, and then slipped a videotape into the machine underneath it. He pressed 'play'. "This is the project I'm working on for English. It probably contains the last recorded dance appearance of Celine Laporte."

Jenna recognized her immediately, even though the camera wasn't trained on her face. Those long thin caramel coloured arms and legs, that simple grace – Celine Laporte was beautiful.

"Her heart failure is a result of anorexia nervosa," Matt reminded Jenna.

The camera moved upwards suddenly and there was that face; bones that seemed to stick out through the skin, eyes that were huge, almost hollow-looking. Wait a minute! Those weren't Celine Laporte's eyes that Matt had on video. Celine's eyes were green. These eyes were brown. Jenna squirmed.

The camera panned to another dancer then.

Ahh, that was Celine Laporte. This dancer had green eyes. Jenna relaxed for a moment but then squirmed again. Then who was that other person? The camera panned back. Now Jenna saw the hair, the mini braids all tucked into a neat bun. Jenna wore her hair like that, Jenna had brown eyes. That dancer was *her*!

And she found she liked that person dancing on the screen. She looked graceful and thin, exactly like Celine Laporte. Only Celine might be dying. The thought came back to her and chilled her.

"Jenna, Celine was a great, great dancer but she'll probably never dance again. Look at her, look at you. Don't you want to grow up and have the chance to dance professionally?"

Jenna could only nod.

"I know you hate me for this but I just can't stand by any longer. You're sick and you don't even know it. We have to tell someone. We need to get you help."

Jenna wanted to strike out at him, to yell out no, that she was strong, that she had control. But everything inside her felt as if it was sliding. She felt weak and tired and sick of fighting with everyone, sick of being afraid of food, sick of thinking about eating. "I don't know what to do."

"Mum went to pick up your grandmother. She was the only one at home."

"Nana?" she asked out loud. Suddenly the image of a different, younger grandmother came to her mind. She remembered Nana holding her hand as they sat mesmerized watching *Giselle*. She heard herself asking her, "Do you think I can be a ballerina when I grow up?" and Grandma answering, "Baby girl, you can be whatever you set your mind to be." *Don't you want to grow up?* Matt had just asked her. Growing taller and bigger interfered with ballet and if she couldn't dance, did she want to go on? It was all too confusing for her. Suddenly, she needed her nana so badly; she knew she could rely on her to help sort things out.

The door opened and she heard footsteps coming down the stairs. Still she sat on the couch weeping, watching as the video continued and she saw her own feet pounding along with the The Tribal Beat.

"Jenna!" her grandmother called and rushed over to her. Her big arms wrapped around Jenna and for that half moment, Jenna felt a little less frightened. "Nana, I can't do it anymore. I can't..."

"Don't you think about anything right now, Girl Child. Nana's taking you to Dr Worden right away. She's going to get us counselling, or whatever it takes."

☆

Two weeks later, because Jenna had gained the small amount of weight Dr Worden had insisted on, Jenna's counsellor gave her special permission to dance in *The Red Shoes* film shoot which had also been delayed.

Shawn Siamon spoke to the performers beforehand. "We'll be using the empty spotlight technique. Celine Laporte is still in intensive care but if you can imagine her dancing right there," he pointed to the centre of the set and a crew member directed a spotlight to it, "this is the way she wants everyone to remember her anyway. And if you dance your absolute best...then I'm sure this scene will be a credit to all of us, including Miss Laporte."

Jenna chewed her lip as she stared at the sad, lonely circle of light.

The set was crowded as the entire crew, from wardrobe mistress to set designer, gathered to watch the scene.

Jenna pirouetted with the others in the wild frenzy Jared Wesker had rehearsed with them so often. No one had trouble keeping a smile from their face as they all focused their eyes on the spotlight – Celine Laporte's light. Jenna imagined Celine in it, so graceful, so beautiful. But she wasn't there and probably never would be again.

"And cut!" the assistant director called. "Very, very nice," she whispered and turned away. A camera operator buried his head in his arms, another paced up and down. Most of the crew was subdued. Jenna walked over to Nana who hugged her and then sat down with her in the extras area, while Jenna choked down a vegetable juice.

"I feel awful, Nana," Jenna told her.

"It will get better again," Nana said as she patted her back. "I promise you. With each day that passes, things will become a little easier."

For Jenna, eating was still torture, but the counsellor's suggestion that she might have to give up ballet entirely had been too much to bear. "Sometimes when we take away the stressful situation, be it ballet, gymnastics or athletics, the patient recovers completely with no recurrence." Now Jenna had a new diet prescribed by a nutritionist and much as she hated to eat all the food on it, she forced herself to do so. It was that or no ballet.

☆

The following week, Matt stood alongside Jenna in front of the English class ready to present his project. Alone, he just hadn't been able to put the words together, but Jenna had come through for him, helping him write the narrative script as well as sharing the reading of it as a voiceover. Her contribution would count towards her English grade but it counted much more in Matt's heart. They were true partners again.

Matt cleared his throat. "Originally I had trouble coming up with a theme for this video. I mean, I thought beautiful dancing was enough to keep anyone's attention." He turned and grinned nervously at Jenna, reaching for her hand.

"But now, with Celine Laporte still in hospital…" Matt's grin dissolved and he hesitated until Jenna nodded and smiled her encouragement, squeezing his hand. He cleared his throat again. "Well, anyway, I've titled this piece *Living to Dance*."

Matt signalled to Headbanger who switched off the classroom lights as Matt pressed the 'play' button. All the scenes Matt had videotaped had been shuffled and re-recorded in the editing suite at Cablecity. Now the first scene was the South

African step dancing clip. Jenna's voice spoke over it. *"Dance can lift your soul, make you laugh, make you happy."*

The camera focused on Matt's smiling face as he competed with Jenna in his rhythmic stomping.

"It's about passion..."

Now, scenes from the Hollywood dancers performing *The Red Shoes* number in Shawn Siamon's film played across the television screen. Byron Jenson had arranged permission for Matt to show it.

"...not being thin," Matt's voice clicked in, finishing the sentence as the heavier-looking dancers pirouetted on screen.

The students watching gasped as Celine Laporte's face filled the screen next. *"In the early history of ballet only men danced. Imagine if this rule had continued. Female dancers only became popular during the early nineteenth century.*

"Of course then black ballet dancers were unheard of. Imagine if this had continued, we would never have had Celine Laporte. What a loss for the world."

The camera followed Celine as she floated across the screen, her face and body as serene as a swan on a lake. This was the first part of *The Red Shoes* before the young girl in the story discovered she could neither remove the shoes nor stop dancing.

"There were times when it was considered beautiful to be heavier." The camera switched back to the 1947 film of *The Red Shoes*. *"For some*

reason, we now like our dancers to be tiny, short and thin." The scene flashed back to Celine, now whirling across the screen in the frenzied dance that was at the end of *The Red Shoes. "What a loss for the world."* Matt's voice sounded like a tortured sigh.

On the screen an empty spotlight floated. *"Can't a tall woman look beautiful beside a shorter partner? Can a heavy person not dance gracefully? What about a person with a disfigured face? What colour is beauty? What size?"*

The last scene was playing on the television as Jenna took over the narration. *"Who decides what height a great dancer can be? Who decides what colour, what size? Who decides what is beautiful?"*

On screen, Matt and Jenna performed their scholarship-winning dance, first leaping over imaginary parking meters and then acting out their struggle against imaginary barriers. Imaginary barriers; they weren't real at all, Jenna thought. She was so grateful to Matt for helping her to see that. She smiled, watching the video as she listened to herself.

"We decide who is beautiful, what colour, what size. We decide who can dance." On the television set Matt and Jenna burst from their choreographed walls trapping them. *"I believe that we decide who we can be. Everyone who works hard enough can be anything they want. Starving to dance is a crime against art and humanity. Nobody should do this."*

As she listened, Jenna remembered labouring

over these words with Matt, writing them, rewriting them, reading them and rereading them. But the meaning of the words hadn't really sunk in. It had all just been for a school mark. She hadn't felt well enough then to believe in the words. But at last she was feeling a little better, and her mind was clearing again. She was eating with the gang in the canteen – only small meals, it was true, but she wasn't screeching at the first sign of food, Caribbean or not. Now she listened to her words on the voiceover with a sense of hope and joy. She smiled as she believed her grandmother's words again. *You can be whatever you set your mind to be*.

She looked over at Matt and he gave her a thumbs up sign. She remembered a time when she thought he wasn't serious enough about dance. She thought about how quickly she'd abandoned him when he had been ill with the 'kissing disease'. Was it only two weeks ago when she'd hated him for interfering in her dieting – when she thought he was ruining her life? Matt had been a true friend, seeing her through a very dark period in her life. Now she felt bound to him forever. Partners in soul as well as in dance.

She gave him a thumbs up sign back and smiled. On screen, they were holding hands and bowing. They looked like the perfect couple. Could they be? Or were they just the best of friends? Would they dance together professionally? Or would Matt continue to struggle with glandular fever as she did with anorexia? Her own voice answered her from the speakers on the television set.

"I am going to be a ballet dancer. Whether I'm tall, black or size medium. This is what I have decided. I have to be healthy to do this and to eat normally. I have to get better. I will get better. Everything is possible if you set your mind to it."

Matt wasn't sure he should applaud his own video, but when Jenna grinned and gave a little bow at the end he couldn't help himself. He wanted to clap for her amazing recovery. He continued clapping because she was his beautiful partner and through all the hard times he would stick by her. And he also clapped because just before presenting the film Jenna had agreed to go out with him – for a pizza.

Preview the next

STAGE SCH★★L

NOW...

Dan - Double Drama

☆CHAPTER ONE☆

The Moon and the Sun

Today was the day, Dan decided, as he strolled from the front door of his apartment building. He was finally going to ask Nikki out officially. As if in encouragement, a million swallows started to twitter at him from a tree. Dan whistled back at them as he swung his court jester's hat in the air, the bells decorating the ends jingling.

Nikki would be his first real girlfriend, assuming of course that she said yes. He'd had a big crush on Abbi, his acting partner, since auditioning for his place at William Holly School – only she'd never felt the same way about him. But Nikki did, he felt almost sure.

Dan broke into a light jog. For once in his life everything was going smoothly. He'd tried out for his first really serious Shakespeare role and Mr Steel, the drama teacher, hadn't laughed. His grades were good, at 'Hollywood High', as the students affectionately called their performing arts school, and Dan felt he belonged; he no longer got into trouble all the time for being the class clown. One of his father's novels was on the *New York Times* Bestseller list, so food and money were plentiful these days. And then there was Nikki...

Dan leapt up, grabbing at an overhanging branch...Nikki – the beautiful petite artist who had transferred from Central Tech High when the school had burned down... He sighed as his feet hit the path again, his hand clutching a few leaves from the tree above him. When Nikki's soft brown eyes looked up at him, he knew he could conquer the world! With her at his side, that Shakespeare role was his! He couldn't wait to ask her out. Only he still had an hour to kill before she'd be free from baby-sitting for her younger brother and sister.

He decided to browse around his favourite joke shop, The What Store, while he waited. From the standard plastic vomit, and buzzing handshake buttons, to the more exotic singing toilet paper – and today a remote control gorilla that followed him from the moment he walked through the door – The What Store carried everything for the practical joker.

"Hey Dan, how do you like King Kong?" the assistant asked him. Most of the salespeople there knew him by name.

Dan smiled as the gorilla performed a back flip.

"Have you seen these yet?" The young woman grabbed a fuzzy ball with a face and flung it to the ground. *"Ouch! Hey stop that!"* a disgruntled mechanical voice growled.

"Great, eh?" The assistant grinned.

Dan nodded.

"Can I help you with anything today?" She flung another furry ball against the counter and this one growled *"Bombs away!"*

"No, thank you." Dan spun the windmill on the top of the beanie hat that was on display. "I've actually just tried out for a serious part."

"Really? Then you need something for good luck." The clerk held up a large rubber chicken by its neck. "You can't beat old Henny Penny here. You're bound to get the part."

Dan shook his head wistfully. "She's great. But too big to carry around, especially when you want to be taken seriously."

"The mini-Henny works just as well," she said, holding out a smaller, yellow chicken keyring.

"How can I resist." Dan counted out his money and took away his good luck chicken feeling even more confident than before.

Next door to The What Store was the Unicorn Shop – a trinket and jewellery store all the girls at school seemed to like. He stopped and looked at the window display.

The lucky chicken was working. There in the window sat the perfect present for Nikki. A brooch – a silver moon and a golden sun laughing together on a cloud. Dan wanted to give her a special gift, now that they were about to be officially dating. He rushed in and bought it for her. Then he glanced at his watch. Half an hour early. He decided to take his chances and head over to Nikki's house anyway.

When he heard the shouting through the front door, with the baby wailing in the background, he wondered if it had been such a great idea. Nikki arrived flustered at the door, her pouty-faced brother Kevin beside her. Her brown eyes looked ready to overflow and Kevin was snuffling into the elbow of his shirt.

Dan acted quickly. "What's causing these sniffles? Do you have something up your nose?" With a slight of hand, he produced one of his own red balls from Kevin's nose. It was a trick he'd learned from his Christmas job with the Lillith Singers and it never failed to get a smile from children. "How can you hear with this in your ear?" he asked Nikki, as he pulled another ball from her ear. Then he began coughing and pretended to spit up a third ball into his hand. "It must be an epidemic," he told them and started juggling the balls.

Nikki smiled at him. "Come on in, Dan." Then she added in a whisper, "Don't mind my parents. My dad flunked another interview and came home with a new CD player."

Dan frowned sympathetically as he caught the balls one by one. Then he followed Nikki to the living room and proceeded to teach Kevin to juggle. "You practise that while we're gone. Next time, I'll show you how to produce those balls from your nose by yourself." He winked at him.

When he finally stepped out of the door again

with Nikki, he couldn't wait a moment longer. At the first bus stop, he sat her down on the bench. Then he cleared his throat, and brushed away one of Nikki's dark spikes of hair from her face. "I really like being with you, Nikki, and I'd like us to be going out officially. I bought this as a symbol." Dan reached into his pocket and the chicken keyring tumbled out.

Nikki giggled.

"No, not the rubber chicken... That's to help me get the part I want. This!" He reached into his pocket again and produced a small box.

When she opened it, Nikki gasped, "It's beautiful, Dan!"

"They're like you and me," he said, "happy to be as different as night and day." And he pinned it on her jacket. Then he kissed her gently. He took Nikki over to a photo booth in the market, and had their pictures taken, together and separately. To capture the perfect moment.

Dan and Nikki have just started dating, and they're very happy together. But for how long? There's trouble in paradise when artistic differences over the school production of Hamlet cause problems and heartache. Read on in...

Stage School 11
☆Dan – Double Drama☆

Have you read the other Stage School stories?

STAGE SCHOOL ★☆

"Just like real life, but loads more exciting!"

MEET THE CAST!

MATT - Dancer

Hunky Matt is Hollywood High's very own heartbreaker...and he knows it! His complicated love life involves two girls, but who does he really want to date? He's also a very talented dancer...when he's not kidding around. But not everything's so easy for him: his health problems are affecting his dancing. And his parents have trouble understanding his dancing ambitions.

LAUREN - Singer

Shy Lauren has a wonderful classical singing voice. But she never feels that she quite fits in properly: after all, she didn't really plan to come to William S. Holly. But she's gradually finding her feet and, with the help of her friends, settling in. However, her parents don't approve of stage school. Lauren is in love with Matt, but is she the right girl for him?

ABBI - Actress
A tumble of blonde curls and a whirlwind of energy. Abbi has an amazing stage presence and expresses her emotions with her whole body. She gets excited really easily, and is scatty, dizzy, lovable and funny, but she tends to hog centre stage!

JENNA - Dancer
Jenna's a beautiful and talented dancer. But she doesn't fit into the traditional ballerina mould in more ways than one. She feels she has to compensate by working extra hard. She has no time for anything else, especially relationships. So it often seems as though dance has taken over her life!

DAN - Actor
Dan's the class clown, always ready with a joke for every occasion. His off-the-wall sense of humour, creativity and sense of fun make him popular amongst his friends. And his love life is finally coming together! Secretly, Dan wants to be a serious actor but his looks and presence type-cast him as a comedian. And Dan's home life is no piece of cake: his dad's a writer and money is sometimes short.

ABBI – MAKE OR BREAK

Stage School is going to be TOTALLY brilliant. But the auditions are soooo tough. Jenna's sure to get in - she's a fantastic dancer. I'm not sure about Chloe - she's weird! Dan's a real comedian, but who could take him seriously? I really hope we all make it - this is all we've ever wanted and you only get one chance...

It's audition time at William S. Holly Stage School, known as 'Hollywood High'. Follow Abbi and a group of other hopefuls as they face the gruelling auditions...share in the excitement of success, and the disappointment of failure.

ISBN 1 86039 642 9   £2.99

ABBI – BLIND AMBITION

Blair Michaels is my favourite TV star and I want to be just like her! But what are Jenna and Lauren so HUFFY about? Are they jealous because she's noticed me? I don't want to lose my old friends, but Blair can help me get a BIG part in Dracula! And who knows I could end up on TV!!!

There's great excitement – the school's putting on a musical version of *Dracula*! But will Abbi get a lead part? She's made a new friend, but the rest of the gang are not so sure about Blair's true intentions, especially when she promises to help Abbi get the part she wants. Will Abbi discover the real reason for Blair's friendship before it's too late?

ISBN 1 86039 643 7 £2.99

JENNA – DANCING DREAMS

I want to be a dancer and I'm prepared to do whatever it takes to succeed. You need to work really hard - there's no time for anything else in your life. So why do people keep trying to change me? I don't want to be a model. And I DON'T want to dance with that maddening Matt!

Dancing means everything to Jenna. But it feels like everyone around her is trying to pull her away from it - her mother and sister want her to become a model, and Matt just wants to fool around. How will Jenna be able to win the New York dance scholarship without their support?

ISBN 1 86039 644 5 £2.99

LAUREN – DRASTIC DECISIONS

I have to face facts. I don't belong at Stage School. I'm not like Matt or Abbi - they're not scared of anything. Matt's never going to notice a mouse like me. I love singing, but maybe I should leave Stage School just like my parents want. The others probably won't even notice I've gone!

Torn between two worlds, Lauren has to decide to do either what her parents want and train to be an opera singer, or to follow her heart and stay at stage school. In the process she finds a friend in a young homeless boy whom she tries to help with surprising results!

ISBN 1 86039 645 3 £2.99

DAN – CLOWNING AROUND

No, not ketchup sandwiches again! I've got to earn some money and fast. I'm tired of hiding my problems behind a joke. Suddenly the local clown has got to get serious!

Everyone's caught up with the auditions for the *Zit-Be-Gone* commercial. No one notices that things are not going very well for Dan. Always the joker, Dan's now in trouble because his real life problems are no laughing matter. Then there's Abbi, whom he really likes, but who just won't take him seriously...

ISBN 1 86039 646 1   £2.99

MATT – HEARTBREAK HERO

What's happening to me? I've never been ill in my life and suddenly I'm in hospital. And now my dad's on my back, Jenna's gone cold and the school's in trouble. One way or another this could be the end of my dancing career...

Matt's got a lot on his plate – keeping up with his dancing and his Saturday job at his dad's shop. When he falls seriously ill, he has to make decisions about what matters to him most. And, it looks as though the stage school might have to close down because of lack of funds. Will the kids be able to pull together and find a way to save it?

ISBN 1 86039 647 X £2.99

LAUREN – DREAM DATING

Life is looking up! I've got an audition to sing in a film IF my dad gives me permission – he still wants me to be an opera singer. And I THINK Matt likes me, although he hasn't asked me out yet. Maybe he still likes Jenna, or Martha.
I wish I knew for sure...

Does Matt fancy Lauren? He seems to, but is the school heart-throb ready to settle down with just one girl? Will Lauren ever get to be the singing sensation she has always dreamed of being, or will her parents stand in her way?

ISBN 1 86039 895 2   £2.99

NIKKI – STOLEN DREAMS

What's a REAL artist like me doing stuck here at Stage School? These kids couldn't tell a Picasso from a pizza. Still, one or two of them are OK. Dan's kind of cute, but he'll never have anything to do with me if he knows what I've done...

Nikki's one of the new 'artsy fartsy' students who have just arrived at William S. Holly. But some of her actions are definitely suspicious, according to Abbi. Then, a school camera goes missing. Is Nikki the thief? The gang investigates!

ISBN 1 86039 896 0   £2.99

ABBI – SECRET STRANGER

Someone is starting fires all over the city. I'm sure I know who it is, but I don't have any proof... And I'm having a tough time in mime class. Dan's supposed to be helping me, but he's spending all his time with Nikki. Dan's JUST a friend, he's the class clown... so why am I jealous of Nikki?

An arsonist has started a number of fires all over the city. Abbi has her suspicions about the culprit… Meanwhile, the gang have to find a way to save the Maxwell Theatre. Perhaps they can look for the fire-bug when they perform on the street to raise money?

ISBN 1 86039 897 9   £2.99

DAN - DOUBLE DRAMA

Things are going great with Nikki. I've finally found a girl who loves me for what I am. But she doesn't understand my acting – I have a chance to prove to everyone that I can be a serious actor, and Nikki's ruining it! With all the special effects she wants for the set we're all going to be laughed off the stage!

Dan and Nikki have finally got it together and are officially dating! But for how long? There's trouble in paradise when artistic differences over the school production of Hamlet cause problems.

ISBN 1 86039 899 5   £2.99

ABBI – ON LOCATION!

I'm SO EXCITED about going to New York! I'm going to be a film extra! Jenna and Matt are coming too, for a dance workshop. PLUS, I'll be meeting my dad for the first time in four years! I REALLY hope Dan'll come too... OK, so he's dating Nikki, but he's still MY best friend!

Is Dan coming to New York too?
The Big Apple holds quite a few surprises
for Abbi. Her meeting with her Dad is not
quite the way she imagined it to be, and
she finds romance... in an unlikely place.
Is reckless Abbi finally growing up?

ISBN 1 86039 900 2   £2.99